TRUMPLAND

DIVIDED

WE

STAND

This is a work of **fiction**.

While public figures, persons, and places are named, they are used fictitiously, in line with fictitious events and incidents and are products of each author's imagination – no matter how bad you may want them to be true.

All other names, characters, places, and incidents are the products of the author's imagination and any resemblance to actual persons (living or dead), companies, events, organizations, or locations is purely coincidental.

<u>WARNING</u>:

While this is a work of fiction, we would like to advise you, the reader, of various triggers contained within the stories you are about to explore. The triggers include reference or depictions of violence both in mass and in individual terms as well as reference or depictions of abuse, sexual and physical, in mass and in individual terms.

We have done our best to be gentle while still telling the stories we felt needed to be told. Please, as you read these them, remember your own self-care and self-worth. We are here with you, in these stories, and some moments were as hard to write as they may be to read. So, take your time, the words will always be here, and we will be here too, when you're ready.

CONTENTS

"We won with the poorly educated,

I love the poorly educated,"

Donald Trump – 2016

The Voice of America

By: Jay Bower

Good morning citizen! Prepare to do your best today. Your country needs you!

Justin pressed his temple, turning off the alarm. The message never changed. Neither did the wake-up time. 6am. Every day. EVERY FREAKING DAY. The moment he was placed on first shift, the structure for his life was set. He had hoped to get second shift so he could sleep longer, but that wasn't his lot.

Throughout his small apartment no larger than an office cubicle, machines screamed to life as the new National Anthem of the Very Best Nation greeted him to a new day. Inside his head, the Voice of America commenced with the Presidential greeting.

Welcome to a new day. It's gonna be huge! I mean, just huge! It's the biggest day. Are you ready to give it everything you've got? I'm counting on you. Let's continue to make America Great!

A rush of energy flowed through Justin; a nano-shot given by the device implanted within him. It was better than coffee; some people called it covfefe. He preferred that name over "nano-shot."

It took exactly four minutes to clean up and dress before he left the metallic white apartment cube. The hallway of the building was illuminated with a faint orangish glow, meant to symbolize the greatness of the past and current Presidents. It always made Justin think of powdered drink mix or fungal spores, both preferable to the truth. He heaved slightly but held his stomach in check. It was a sign of weakness to purge before a breakfast of cheeseburgers and diet cola.

He boarded the elevator and rode the thirty-four flights down to the cafeteria, where he joined the lengthy queue for his morning rations. The citizen in front of him, an older Asian man with a scar on his left cheek, smiled at him. His white jumpsuit was marked with a red "X" indicating he was a natural born citizen and could stay in the country. Justin's suit had no such markings. He was Caucasian and traced his lineage to decades before the First Election thirty years ago.

Justin smiled back. "Good morning!" He said cheerfully. There was nothing particular to be happy about, but he often felt it lifted the mood if he at least acted the part. The man nodded, his grin growing larger.

"Ready to make America great again?" Justin asked.

The man nodded sheepishly, his grin never fading from his face.

"Can you speak?"

The man nodded again but seemed oblivious. The line moved slowly forward, and Justin said nothing else to the man who continued to grin madly at him.

The orange glow of the cafeteria was contrasted by the long lines of people dressed in white jumpsuits, all of them part of the first shift and ready to perform their constitutional duties. Neglecting to follow orders and work where assigned brought the

Very Good Guys (or VGGs) to your home. No one wanted that.

Justin was humming to himself and trying to make the best of the morning when an alarm blared in his brain. He winced at the sudden outburst and noticed everyone else around him doing the same.

You are in the presence of a terrible person. Someone among you has foreign blood within them. This is bad. Report anyone suspicious to the nearest Very Good Guy. Let's make sure to keep our nation pure.

The Voice of America clicked off and everyone stared at the people nearest them as if to find the evil cancer and rip it out. Justin turned to the Asian man who hadn't stopped grinning.

"Oh no," he whispered. "It's you isn't it?" The man nodded and grinned.

Justin debated his next move. If he said anything, the man was as good as dead. If he said nothing, he ran the risk of a VGG visit. Most didn't live to tell of those visits.

Watching the man blithely move in line toward the morning cheeseburgers, he felt sorry for him. Whatever drew him to the nation and to the center of the country in St. Trump must have been important enough to risk his life. He'd not be the reason the man died today, so he remained quiet.

In a line on the far side of the room, a fight broke out and citizens accosted a man with a blue "X" on his chest, the mark indicating he was of Middle Eastern descent but born in the country naturally. The VGGs were on him fast, the four guards dressed in black clubbing him with their nightsticks. The man screamed out, but no one helped him, instead moving back from the scrum. It didn't take long before the VGGs dragged his bloody and lifeless body from the room.

A click indicated another incoming message.

No more distractions. Work must be done. America needs you. I need you.

When the Voice of America ended, Justin sighed. He'd heard talk of a small band of rebels who removed their implants and lived a life free of the President. From time to time, he considered joining them. Raised to respect the government and listen to all commands, lately his conscience spoke to him in a more powerful voice.

Was it right to murder citizens because they were from a different country? Did skin color really make a difference?

In high school he had a friend from East St. Trump, just across the Mississippi River. His dark skin drew a lot of unwanted attention. He was the best friend Justin ever had, until a girl from school falsely accused him of being a traitor. VGGs came in the middle of the night and dragged him away. He was never seen again.

When Justin confronted her, she smiled. "He got what he deserved. All he had to do was kiss me. Damn queer wouldn't even do that."

"That's wrong!" he screamed back at her. "What you did was wrong! Who cares who he likes? He's not done anything to anyone."

"Whatever. He should've been into girls, like a normal boy."

Rage built within but he kept it in check. Lashing out only meant giving in to the hate.

He regretted his inaction ever since. Now, witnessing the latest abuse, it only crystallized in his mind what needed to be done.

Justin tapped the small implant on the side of his head and turned on the radio. Music instantly blossomed in his brain, drowning out the mayhem of the moment. He tapped along to the music on his leg, keeping an eye on the Asian man in front of him and hoping to escape the notice of the VGGs.

The line continued moving forward and cheeseburgers and diet cola were handed out quickly by the cafeteria workers. The Asian man ahead of Justin received his meal, still flashing his suspicious grin. The worker must not have noticed, or cared, and waved him on when the transaction was over.

"Rough morning, huh?" Justin asked. The music continued to blare in his brain but neglecting to show deference to anyone in authority was grounds for a VGG visit.

"People need to know their place. If they aren't from here, this is not their place."

Justin nodded absently and sat to eat his rations.

After breakfast, he scurried out of the cafeteria to make the train for work. He couldn't be late again.

The ride lasted fifteen minutes. By the time he disembarked, he'd already listened to three songs interspersed with edicts from the President.

There was no escape from the Voice of America. Unless…

He blasted the thought from his mind, worried that somehow the mere inkling of a thought could be caught by the implant. Some speculated that the government knew everything about its citizens through the Voice of America, that it somehow tapped into the host body and intercepted thoughts and feelings. That was how the VGGs were nearly unstoppable, they said.

He made it to work on time. Baseball caps needed to be made; America was only as great as the number of caps handed out at rallies. When production was brought back in from China after the Great Trade Void, factories were commissioned across the country. This one on Delmar Street in St. Trump was the largest in Missouri and enjoyed special favor from the government because of their efficiency and nearly all Caucasian workforce.

Halfway through the morning shift, Justin chanced alerting the VGGs by letting his mind wander to freedom. *What would it be like to never hear commands in my head?* he thought. The Voice was always there, always mocking, always demanding. Were the rebels, right? Did something better exist out there? Could he unplug?

The events of the morning raced to the forefront and he cringed. The poor man killed in front of everybody--

Hey there! Hello. Oh, hi. Doing well today?

The Voice made Justin jump. Though saddled with the device since birth, it still startled him when the Voice came to life unexpectedly.

I really, really like your good work with the caps. You make me proud and that's a very good thing. It's shameful what some people will do to take your jobs. I won't allow it. We are the greatest nation on the planet. I don't care what those other countries say. You are the best.

The Voice clicked off and Justin noticed those around him swell with pride. He used to feel the same, but something felt...different. The ordeal earlier had bothered him in a deep way, unlike any other time. He rubbed at the device near his temple and turned the music back on. Work needed to be done and his boss would be anxious to crush their quota after the earlier announcement.

The rest of the day passed without another interruption from the Voice, an odd though not entirely without precedent event. It had grown more common lately, but Justin never questioned it.

On the way home, Justin leaned his head against the glass, watching the streets fly by. The Metro was only half-filled and VGGs walked up and down the aisle with guns strapped across their backs. It used to be a comforting sight with them securing the streets. Crime had dropped dramatically, but now they made Justin nervous, as though they were watching and waiting for him to give them a reason to lash out. He'd never done so and carefully lived his life to avoid doing so.

The Metro came to a screeching halt between stations. The hair on Justin's neck stood on end. The Voice of America rang in his head.

What a glorious day today has been. Our friends the North Koreans have finally taken over the entire peninsula and the war is over. The good son of former King Putin, God rest his soul, is stopping by the White House for a chat. Isn't America great? The Wall holds steady to the south, keeping those people away from our jobs and our wonderful way of life. But now, we move into a more dangerous territory. Something very, very bad has come to my attention.

The Voice paused and Justin glanced at everyone else on the train, all eyes wide open paying close attention to the latest edict. Then the Voice continued.

I've been informed of a terrorist organization threatening to ruin our way of life. They are non-purists who pose as citizens in order to avoid detection. They are living among you. They might even be your family members. Report any and all suspicious activities to the nearest Very Good Guys. Remember, I need you to make sure America stays great.

Thankfully the Voice clicked off and the train slowly lurched forward. The latest pronouncement sent shivers down Justin's spine. Didn't anyone else see the ugliness inherent in the government? It was not the country he once thought it was. Maybe the rebels were right after all.

By the time Justin made it home, something had snapped inside him.

He couldn't stop thinking about the man murdered in the morning. The way his friend was stolen and likely killed hadn't left his thoughts all day, despite the possibility of detection. The vile things the Voice of America screamed at him were too much. Justin found himself ready to act in a way he'd never done before. Inaction had meant loss. Doing nothing resulted in innocent people being hurt, or worse. How much longer was he going to sit by and do nothing?

Frantically he scoured his living space for something-- anything--to use. Then he found a rigid piece of wire sticking out from under his cabinet. As he yanked on the metal, it cut deep into his hands.

I don't care. I cannot live like this anymore! he screamed in his head.

Finally, he pulled it free and held it close to his face, turning it around in his hands.

"This'll do," he whispered.

He had no idea where the rebels were or how to contact them. All he knew was that the nightmare had to end. It was too much, no one should have to endure what Americans were dealing with. After he performed the extraction, he'd find some way to return to freedom.

The small mirror above the sink was cloudy, but it provided enough reflection for him to see where he needed to cut. Inhaling deep, he pushed back his hair and held the edge of the wire to his temple. The cold metal pushed against his skin and he hesitated.

Is this the right thing to do? Is there another way?

He thought of the man from the morning and the Voice directing him to spy on his fellow citizens. He thought of his friend from high school and how terrible the nation had become. He no longer wanted to be part of it.

Taking in a deep breath, he pushed the metal wire into his skin.

A searing pain raced across his face and his eye watered. His hand shook. Then the Voice called out into his head.

Citizens! Great, wonderful news! Our friends the Russians have agreed to our demands. Soon we will host one of their missile silos while they agree to purchase American wheat. It's a great day for America! If you would join me--

Justin pushed the wire harder, ignoring the words rattling in his head. Hot searing pain radiated out from the intrusion. Blood trickled down his face. Sweat dripped down his forehead, running along his nose, and across his lips. His breathing intensified. The Voice continued ranting.

We must be vigilant against those who threaten our purity. God demands it. Will you join me in snuffing out the bad guys? You must be prepared to do what's right--

Justin gripped his makeshift cutting implement tightly and slowly dragged it across his skin, opening the wound further. The madness had to stop! This was the only way.

He felt the wire scrape against the bone underneath, the metal scratching its presence within him. He gritted his teeth, unwilling to give up.

Today is one of the bestest days in our nation's history! You are witness to a wonderful series of events. Our forefathers would be proud of the nation we've made! One day--

Justin fought the urge to stop as the metal cut his flesh. Blood ran freely down his face, covering his hand. He pushed on, emboldened by the reality setting in by the rants within his head.

The wire scraped against something metal, and Justin stopped.

"Agh!" he cried out, not caring if his neighbors heard him. Before he could talk himself out of it, he reached in the wound with his fingers, feeling for the small metal device. He brushed against it and the exposed nerves screamed at him.

The Voice within his head rambled on about trade and economics and purity. Justin paid little attention to the words anymore. His focus on the device he now held within his fingertips. Closing his eyes, he pulled on it.

The intense shock made him crumble to the floor. His entire body felt like it was on fire as though thousands of fire ants crawled over his skin and pierced his flesh with their tiny, horrible mouths. He convulsed and beat his head on the hard floor. Blackness invaded his vision, and everything began to fade.

No, he thought, *I'm not done yet!*

Determined more than ever to be rid of the anger constantly flooding his mind, he grabbed hold of the device with his blood-soaked fingers and pulled.

The sound of tearing flesh accompanied his efforts. Despite the torrid pain, he pulled harder. The device ripped from his body. His hand fell to the floor and the small metal implant tumbled out as he passed out.

Sometime later, Justin awoke to a pounding headache reminiscent to the time he got wildly drunk and experienced the worst hangover of his life. The rhythmic thud of his heartbeat within his skull threatened to bore a hole through the bone. He closed his eyes, wishing for the agony to end. But instead, he discovered silence.

He listened intently for the Voice that always intruded on his thoughts and felt an odd loneliness. The Voice of America was so ingrained in his life that it was a part of him. Now, the blood-covered remnants of a past he forcefully excised from his life lay on the floor next to him.

Crusted blood cracked as he sat upright and ran his hands across his face. A pool of dried blood covered the floor next to where his head lay. But the device was gone. No more rants. No more ignorant calls to reprehensible action. Only silence, a void where his own thoughts could, for the first time in his life, emerge and flourish.

*   *   *

Several days passed and Justin remained in his tiny apartment except to eat once a day. Without the Voice directing him, he at first didn't know what to do but soon figured out how to fake his way through the day without attracting too much attention.

He failed to show up for work. His boss sent a letter firing him "Immediately and without pay" as his last paycheck would be used to cover the fine levied by the government for missing their quota. Justin smiled at the thought of his prick of a boss being berated for losing the favor of the government.

A week after he removed the implant, Justin prepared to leave his apartment for the last time. The rebels were out there, and he'd find them. No matter what it took, he'd join their ranks. Without the Voice belittling him and sowing discord, life had grown considerably more bearable.

Closing the door behind him for what he expected was the last time, a familiar voice startled him.

Greetings citizen! We're so happy to have you back. Sometimes we have to do tough things in order to make America Great, and for you, we've done just that. Such a shame you removed the lifetime implant, but no worries! Once your actions came to our attention, we fixed the problem and you're you again.

Justin sank to the hallway floor, clutching his head in his hands.

"No! Fuck you! Get out of my head!"

He was vaguely aware of VGGs approaching, his fury rendering him slow to react.

We've had to engage the emergency comms installed when the original implant was injected. It's all standard stuff. Anyway, by now you'll notice the Very Good Guys are nearby. Don't fight them! They're deadly. One of the hardest working men I have. Soon you'll be back at a job doing great things for America. We need you. I need you. No other President has done for you what I have. Maybe my grandfather Donald, but he's been gone for many years. You're too valuable to us to lose. With my guidance and your obedience, we'll work extra hard to Make America Great...Again!

The Voice of America clicked off. The VGGs yanked him from the floor.

"No, stop! Can't you see how wrong this is?" he cried out. One of the VGGs backhanded him, sending a brilliant flash of light across his vision.

"Pleease, you know this is wrong! We have to fight. We have–"

Another smack across his face knocked a tooth loose, sending it flying across the hall where it slammed against the far wall. The orangish glow of the light made him queasy.

Freedom had been so close. The week of silence created a yearning for something greater than the life America afforded its people. A dark realization seeped into his thoughts, crushing the spirit he emboldened by removing the device: His life was not his own, no matter how hard he wanted to be free. Freedom didn't belong to America anymore. America belonged to the government. And the Voice of America would make sure all the people knew it.

The VGGs dragged him down the hall to a bleak future he had no chance of escaping. Death was his only hope, and that couldn't come soon enough.

About the author

Jay Bower

Jay Bower is a horror author living outside St. Louis, MO in the forest of Southern Illinois. He spends his time reading, writing, and convincing his wife the dark stories he writes do not involve her.

His most recent novel, Useless Creatures, can be found on Amazon.

https://www.amazon.com/gp/product/B07N974BL3

"And when you're talking about an atmosphere, oceans are very small. And it blows over, and it sails over."

Donald Trump - 2018

Poisoned Well

By: Margret A. Treiber

He stumbled through the portal and fell to the ground. The device smoked and sparked behind him, then it completely lost power. Although he appeared uninjured, Myron lay there shaking. He looked older, weathered, and sobbed woefully until Glenna sat next to him and took his hand.

"Did you fail?" she asked. "Are we lost?"

Myron shook his head. "No, I did it." He sucked in a breath, trying to compose himself. "Just as we discussed. I'm afraid I set science back centuries. And the environment..." Myron started sobbing.

"We had no choice." Glenna stroked his back as he cried. He earned this release, having taken the burden of responsibility to do what had to be done.

"So, when we open that door?"

"The world will be unrecognizable." Myron wiped the tears from his face. "We will be backward, petty, ill-informed..."

"...but alive," Glenna added.

Myron nodded. "Yes."

"We'll remember. Somehow we'll recover."

Glenna helped Myron to his feet. They walked up the stairs and stopped at the sealed metal door. Glenna flung it open, revealing a neon jungle full of pollution and despair. On the corner where the old oak tree used to grow, a prostitute hawked her wares. The entire forest was replaced by an expanse of decrepit tenements. The sounds of gunfire rang out in the distance, but there were no explosions.

Myron began to sob again. Glenna squeezed his hand. "It's okay," she said. "You saved us."

*   *   *

It was an ideal day. The post-rain sun peeked through the clouds creating a double rainbow that nearly stopped traffic. Glenna stopped at the food trucks and had a tunarito before heading back to the lab. The climate grant had just been extended for another decade, so she was riding high on the spoils of job security.

"Hi Inez," she said as she entered the building.

Inez barely looked up from the reception desk. "Hello," she replied. She was a few years younger than Glenna and just starting the education phase of her internship.

"What you are studying?" Glenna asked.

"I'm considering a career in theoretical physics," Inez stated. "I'm torn between that and applied chemistry."

"You can always try one and switch if you hate it," Glenna said.

"Yeah, but which one do I pick?" Inez asked. "I know it

doesn't cost anything, but I don't want to lose the time."

"The time isn't lost if you learn something."

"True." The phone rang. "Environmental Studies," Inez answered.

Glenna waved at her and strolled into her office. She sat and quietly sipped her coffee, easing into the day. She liked to catch up on the previous night's events and slowly get into a work rhythm. Pulling up the news feed, Glenna noticed it was surprisingly sparse. It seemed that her page was filled with yesterday's articles. Even though the world was at peace, for the most part, there were always minor skirmishes here and there. Things happened. Even small current events should have updated. But none appeared. It made no sense that there was no new news. Glenna wondered if her newsreader was malfunctioning. She rebooted it to see if it would update. Not only didn't it refresh, but now the feed was completely blank. She'd have to speak to the IT people later, but now there was work to do.

Glenna's tasklist was long, but she didn't mind. She loved her job. Her life was fulfilling, and her work was challenging. She counted herself lucky to be living in this era. Her parents used to tell her how it was before mankind began to embrace science as a whole, when religion and bigotry defined policy and when denial was the order of the day. Now, everyone had the chance to fulfill their ambitions without denying others of their own dreams. Everyone had an equal chance at happiness. Glenna grinned as she sipped her coffee again.

"Glenna." Myron's voice came through Glenna's headset. He was the senior researcher and her boss. "We've found some inconsistencies in your calculations on the sea level rise. Could you recheck your figures?"

"Yes," Glenna answered. "I'll be happy to. I'd rather work on that than deal with my broken newsreader."

"Yeah, mine's out, too. I'll take a look later."

"Thanks, how are you this morning?"

"Tired," Myron replied. "I underwent my physical Tuesday and the doctor put me through my paces."

"Are you alright?" There was concern in Glenna's voice.

"Oh, yeah," Myron answered. "I'm fine. They gave me a full tune-up. I'm feeling twenty-five again."

"So why are you tired, really?"

Glenna could almost hear the sheepish grin through the speaker. "Well, I was feeling so good and I was so behind on the data crunching, I decided to break night catching up."

"You should get some sleep before...." Glenna was interrupted by the sounds of explosions. "What?" It took a moment for her to register what the sound was, and the inherent danger she was in.

The building collapsed around her. She screamed as a chunk of concrete wall bounced off her shoulder. Struggling to get out the door, she scrambled into the lobby. Alarms buzzed and lights flashed. The air was filled with white dust. Glenna trudged through the rubble towards the doors. She saw Inez still seated in her chair.

"Come on," Glenna said. "We need to move."

Inez didn't answer, Glenna reached out and spun the chair around. Inez's face was gone.

Glenna fought the tears as she ran for the door. Once outside she was able to see the source of the destruction. The sky was completely blocked out by large, hovering, alien craft. They were launching weapons at all the buildings.

Myron grabbed Glenna by the arm and pulled her behind an overturned food cart.

"What do we do," she sobbed.

"We get out of the city and wait," he said. "We need to find out what is happening."

Myron found an undamaged day rental vehicle and drove the pair out to the rural sector. He had a small cabin in the woods he used for personal research and when he needed solitude. Fortunately, it was untouched when they arrived.

"It doesn't look like this place was targeted," Myron said.

"Inez is dead," Glenna sobbed.

"Many people are dead," Myron replied. "We need to focus and find out why."

"How can you..."

"Listen, I'm old enough to remember how things were before. You're young and haven't had to live through the kind of adversity we used to endure. It took many of us long years to make the world a safe place for our children, you. But violence was not uncommon when I was a child. I remember. So just follow my lead and we will get through this."

Glenna nodded.

Myron pulled out an old radio from the closet and hooked it up to power. He connected an antenna and began adjusting it. It took some time, but he calibrated the equipment and was able to contact others.

"What's going on?" Glenna asked.

"It looks like they are destroying our civilization. Our government tried negotiating, but they weren't interested. The moment our representatives contacted them, they cut them off and disabled planetary communications."

"My newsfeed..."

"Yes," Myron replied. "They took it all out right before they started the attack on our cities."

"Who are they?"

Myron shook his head. "They're from another world. Life on their planet was destroyed by a gamma-ray burst and they were the only ones off-world when it happened. They've been traveling for years in search of a new pristine planet to start over on. The Earth is clean, biologically diverse and full of resources. They want it, and we can't stop them. We're outgunned."

"So, we're going to die?"

"My friend Mark had an idea. It's experimental, but it may work."

"What is it?" Glenna asked.

"Time travel."

"Time travel is illegal," Glenna stated.

"It's all we have."

"How will time travel help us? We can't stop them from coming. We can't stop their world from dying."

"Yeah, but we can send someone back to change this world. Make it unappealing to them."

"You mean destroy our paradise?"

"Yes." Myron nodded. "Destroy our paradise so we can live.

We need to poison the well."

"How?"

"We'll have to go back to that pivotal time when we started to make the change for good. We need to nudge the world on a path away from enlightenment toward one of the status quo. Let greed and selfishness destroy the environment, so the Earth is useless to them."

A tear rolled down Glenna's cheek as she processed the idea. "Okay, let's do it."

"The time machine isn't far. It's isolated, nestled in the northwest forest, so it's safe. Mark is waiting for us there. We agreed that I'll go through the portal since I'm the oldest and know what to look for."

"You know what to do?"

"Yes," he replied. "I do."

"Is it something horrible?"

Myron nodded. "It's far worse than horrible," he stated. "It's criminal."

"What is it?" Glenna asked.

Myron exhaled and looked away from his apprentice in shame. "Trump," he rasped. "We have to reelect Trump."

About the author

Margret A. Treiber

Margret A. Treiber is a writer and an editor for the speculative fiction humor magazine, Sci-Fi Lampoon. When she is not writing or working at her day job with technology, she helps her birds break things for her spouse to fix.

Her fiction has appeared in several publications.

Links to her short stories, novels, and upcoming work can be found on her website:

 www.the-margret.com

and on Amazon:

www.amazon.com/Margret-A.-Treiber/e/B0052U63BI/

"They're sending people with problems…
They're bringing drugs, they're bringing crime.
They're rapists."

Donald Trump - 2015

Coyote

By: Sarah Walker

The moon was full tonight. He didn't think much about it, only that he needed to get back home. Outside his window the Texas countryside whipped by, a lying shade of indigo mimicking the ocean with its rolling hills. It didn't offer anything to quench one's thirst though. Once you were lost out there, dehydration and sunstroke hit fast. He knew. He saw it all the time with the illegals they arrested or found cooked and dead under a merciless sun.

He shifted gears as he came up on another rise in the two-lane highway and the engine rumbled into low gear. He was jittering so much he knew his back would be screaming by the time he got to the next gas station, the pitted and disused asphalt beneath rocking the pickup back and forth erratically. He wouldn't normally have gone this way but there had been some sort of accident on the interstate, so he was stuck. It was a route he disliked. It felt abandoned.

The radio was tuning in and out, a sharp male voice became audible suddenly.

"And we have to take back America from these immigrants overrunning our borders. It's our land, we worked hard for it!"

You can say that again, brother.

John turned the radio up.

"Those so-called victims at the border? They aren't victims! That's just what the lying democrats what you to think. In fact, they're just criminals, rapists, drug dealers! We need to stop them from invading. Who will protect your daughter when they come? Who will protect…"? The man's voice was suddenly cut off by a blast of static.

John gritted his teeth and frowned.

"Damn it." He muttered as he tried to tune the station back in but try as he might to get his favorite talk show back, he couldn't. It was no use. Still, he punched the buttons in growing irritation, keeping his eyes on the road, hoping the radio would finally tune back in. Suddenly, a strange noise like high pitched howling cut through the static for a second, but then even that was lost in the sea of electric current.

He looked around and saw off to his right the darkness growing, cutting a jagged desert mesa into the night sky in a black against blue geometry. Soon he was driving in shadows, the road winding through the darkness of the mesa. He sighed and turned the radio off. He wouldn't be able to get a station until he was out of the mesa's range anyway. He drummed his hand on the steering wheel and tried to hum a tune, but soon gave up after feeling strangely creeped out by his own cracked whisky voice straining to sound human. He smoked and drank too much, he knew. Working for the Border police took its toll. He shrugged and tried to think of something to entertain him until he could turn the radio back on.

A hitchhiker appeared on the side of the road. Maybe the guy could help him stay awake. Plus, if it was another wetback, he'd get another arrest in for the day.

He pulled over to the side of the road and the figure jogged up to his passenger side. It was an older Mexican man. A thin moustache and goatee highlighted the bony features making the hitchhiker look decidedly coyote like.

"Hey, Jefe, can I get a ride into the next town? My truck's down for the count." The man motioned off into the darkness. John couldn't see a truck.

Probably an illegal. He's obviously lying.

John thought for a second, considering his gun that he kept in his glove compartment, feeling a bit stupid for stopping before he'd had a chance to move it. He assessed the man again. The guy was very small and clearly didn't have a gun. He looked too ragged to have much of anything. His pants were so shredded John couldn't even figure out what color they had been originally, the white t-shirt so worn and thin that John could see the man's dark body beneath.

Not much of a threat. Fuck it.

"Sure thing. Get on in." He opened the truck's door and the man got in. John swallowed a gasp when he saw the man's feet. His passenger had no shoes on, and the toenails were easily an inch long, making the gnarled dirty brown feet look more like claws than human feet.

What the fuck?

The man closed the passenger door. John thought about saying something but decided to stay silent. If the guy was an illegal, he'd know soon enough. He'd deal with that when the time came. John started driving again.

"So, what made you come out here so late?" He tried to sound nonchalant, but his voice sounded tight and nervous. The guy set off all kinds of alarm bells in John's mind. Something here was not right. Not only did the guy look grungy, he smelled weird, almost like a dog.

Maybe I should make him get out.

The man answered, "I'm always out here. This is my land. And how about you? Why are you here?" The man turned and looked at John with irises as black as obsidian. The whites were slightly yellow giving the man a jaundiced cast. The guy wasn't well, John decided. And definitely not a looker. His pockmarked face didn't help the situation.

"Oh. So, you from around here?" John asked as he tried another tactic.

"Yes. My land. My people." John almost balked at that. What the hell did that mean anyway? John took out a cigarette, carefully driving with his free hand to light it. He motioned a question by shaking the now lit cigarette, "You want one?"

The Mexican man shook his head. "No, I don't partake in tobacco. My people do, but I do not."

What the fuck is this with his people? The guys a fruitcake. Fuck, I need to get rid of him.

John shifted and started to ask the guy what his name was when the man started speaking before, he could.

"You whites, you don't know what it is to be from the land. You have forgotten. In fact, you're the outsiders here and yet you don't even know it. It's actually pretty funny when you guys call

Mexicans foreigners when they have been here thousands of years. Why, you Europeans are the new kids here. It's pretty damn funny." The passenger chuckled good naturedly. John felt heat rising in his face.

"What the fuck do you mean by that?"

The man turned and looked at John, his eyes suddenly slits and dangerous. His face twisted into an unidentifiable expression, but then he smiled slyly.

"Well, you do know that Mexicans are Indians, right? That they were here before you? Maybe even here before Europe even existed." The man went back to looking out the window, smiling and calm as could be.

This guys an idiot. Probably an illegal. Fucking commie left wing idiot.

"Well, that's complete nonsense. Mexicans don't belong here. And besides, none of that bullshit matters. We're here now and it's our land and it's the law."

The Mexican man laughed again.

"The law?" The hitchhiker laughed even harder as if the word was the funniest thing he'd ever heard.

"What do you, a man from the city, know about law? The law of the wild? The law of nature? You know nothing. There are laws older than your human laws. Much, much older."

John was getting angry, angrier than he'd been in a long time. It consumed him to the point that at first, he was at a loss for words to respond to such insanity. Finally, the stuck words came spilling out, but they weren't eloquent as he'd hoped. They were just the first words that came to his mind.

"You're a fucking Wetback democrat, aren't you?"

The man laughed again.

"No, no, John. I'm not. Nothing so ..."

"Well, what are you then? What are you saying?" He interrupted the hitchhiker, not yet realizing the man knew his name and should not have.

The man was silent for a moment and then looked at John.

"Times up, John."

John turned to yell at the man when a truck's horn blast stopped him. He'd been so angry at the hitchhiker he'd wandered into the opposite lane. He barely swerved back in time as a giant semi sped past, honking the whole way.

"Fuck me!" The truck began to fishtail as he overcorrected and suddenly the truck was off the road. He felt the vehicle hit something and then flip, his head slamming into the steering wheel.

Then all was blackness.

* * *

As John lay unconscious, the truck didn't stop. His foot was stuck between the gas pedal and the brake and the weight of his unconsciousness kept it floored. Bits of cactus and rock flew up as the truck barreled into a dry and ancient riverbed, the incapacitated driver unaware as the truck kept moving forward, a ghost in the dark. The terrain changed. River rocks now dotted the arroyo. They pinged and clattered against the undercarriage. A sudden sharp metallic screeching noise cut through the night as one of the stones ripped open the belly of the vehicle. Finally, the truck stopped.

*   *   *

Slowly his consciousness faded back in like the lost radio station finally catching a signal. He let his eyes flicker open. He couldn't see, his eyes stung, and nausea washed over him in waves. He sat there for a moment, shaking and close to throwing up, trying to clear his vision, confused as to what had happened and where he was. Finally, his mind started to clear, and he understood why he couldn't see. Something was in his eyes. He reached up and felt it, his hand coming away smeared with blood. He turned on the overhead light and looked at himself in the busted rearview mirror. A million shattered faces met his gaze, blood running down each of their pale white foreheads.

The hitchhiker.

He looked over to the passenger side. It was empty, but the door was closed.

He should never have picked that guy up. What the hell had he been thinking? Where had he gone?

"Fuck!" His anger at migrants, at Mexicans in general, surfaced. It was a great black octopus of a thing swimming in the dark subconscious of his mind and when it awoke....

He stopped himself. He forced a deep breath. Anger wasn't going to help him get through this situation. One thing at a time. How the hell was he going to get out of this arroyo? He took another deep breath and patted his body clumsily. Nothing else seemed to be hurt, just his head. He probably had a concussion. He uncurled his hands from the steering wheel, his knuckles popping with overexertion. He needed to clear his thoughts but try as he might everything was foggy and surreal. He needed to get to a hospital.

He turned the key to the truck in hopes it would turn over, but only a small click came. The headlights flickered for a second and then brightened. He should probably turn them off before he did kill the battery, but he couldn't bring himself to do it. He didn't like it here, wherever here was. And in the dark, he was sure he'd like it less.

Somewhere a wolf howled. Or was it a coyote?

He shivered and swallowed dryly, as he tried to wipe the still running blood out of his eyes, his forehead aching with the wound. The creature howled again, a yipping ending the lonesome arc of song.

They won't come near the truck, just calm down.

He'd better regroup for a moment and figure out what the hell he was gonna do. He sat there for some time, though he couldn't be sure how long. Soon the coyotes were gone, or at least had fallen silent, and he decided he'd better look at the truck and figure out why it wouldn't start.

He slowly got out of the truck, standing for a moment as nauseating dizziness rushed over him again. Finally, he regained his bearings and he began to carefully walk down the length of truck. He couldn't see much in the shadowed arroyo, but he could see the truck wasn't in as bad of shape as he'd first thought. True it was banged up a little and the front grill was dented, but it didn't look too bad considering the wreck. He'd flipped, hadn't he?

He realized he could smell gasoline.

"Shit..."

That's why it won't start.

He walked over to where the gas tank was on the bottom and looked under the car. A huge tear traveled across the whole undercarriage. Gas spilled onto the rocks, slowing now that most of it had been bled away.

"Shit!" His voice slurred a little, but he ignored it. Had to be tough in situations like these. He walked back to the driver's side and got in and closed the door.

The phone!

He had forgotten about it in his injured state. He rummaged through his jacket and finally found the little flip phone. He took it out and began to dial 911. He put the phone up to his ear, Nothing. He looked at it perplexed and then noticed there were no bars. Hope of help arriving anytime soon drained away. He couldn't get a signal.

He tossed the phone onto the seat and let his head fall as he tried to think of what he was going to do. That's when he heard something. He looked up and saw someone looking at him from behind a saguaro cactus.

At first, he thought it was just the cactus but when it moved, he realized it was not the plant, but a young girl. She wore a sackcloth dress that was too big for her. Though her eyes were hidden behind black hair hanging limply over her darkened face, he could feel her staring at him.

 It bothered him. Why would a young girl be put in the middle of the desert in the middle of the night? Where the hell had she come from? Unless…

Someone banged on his passenger window and he almost screamed in surprise. He turned and saw an old Mexican woman. She looked at him as if sizing him up, her face as wrinkled as a prune, her hair done in braids that hung down the sides of her small body. She looked as if she was about to say something but suddenly her eyes narrowed. She turned to the young girl and motioned. They both began to walk away very quickly.

"Hey! Border Patrol! I need help! Alto ahora! Policia! Stop right there!" But they didn't listen, once the girl joined the older woman, they moved much quicker than he'd thought was possible, vanishing into the night and out of range of his headlights as silent and as black as smoke. Soon they were gone into the surrounding darkness.

Must have been illegals with clothing like that out here in the middle of nowhere. Probably know Mr. Democrat Wetback...

Anger flashed through him. He couldn't believe they hadn't stopped and helped him when he'd told them to. He was border patrol after all. *He was the law.* He popped open his glove box and took out his service revolver and his flashlight. He'd go after them, make them help him. They'd have to know where the hell they were and where the nearest town was where he could get help. He'd get them to tell him and then he'd turn them in the first chance he got.

Fucking illegals.

He jumped out of the truck and stood wobbling back and forth for a second. He regained his balance and started to head to the side of the arroyo, adrenaline coursing through him at the prospect of a chase. He tried to run up the side of the arroyo, almost slipping when his head spun around again Merry-Go-Round like for a moment. He couldn't run. He stopped again and waited until it passed.

After a bit he carefully slogged up the sandy embankment and was greeted by a landscape almost as bright as day. Cold white moonlight spilled across the barren land illuminating the rugged desert. He scanned the horizon. In the distance he watched as the figures as they vanished into a depression in the distant scrabble.

"Got you, you fucking bastards." He walked and then ran as best he could, but it was slow going. He kept having to stop to wait for the dizziness to pass every few hundred feet and by the time he'd gotten to the dip in the land, he was panting. He came up the rise and was greeted by an adobe structure below.

It was built next to another sandstone outcropping that grew up out of the earth. Where had it come from? He was sure he'd gone this way before, hadn't he? Maybe he just hadn't seen the structure from the road? He turned around and looked for the two-lane highway, feeling stupid it had just occurred to him to look for it. It was nowhere in sight. He realized with a sinking feeling he had no idea where he was. How the hell could that be? He hadn't gone that far from the road when he'd crashed, had he?

He looked down again at the adobe.

He needed to go down there. He had no way to get his truck out of the ditch, no cell phone, and his head was beginning to spin again. And though he wasn't sure how smart it would be to go down there, what choice did he have? A low growl came from behind him, breaking the ambient silence of the desert night. He spun around, panning his flashlight across the dirt and rocks holding his gun pointed out and ready to fire. His light hit something that moved, so he panned back. It was a coyote, a big one. It watched him with uncomfortable interest, the yellow eyes catching his flashlight and glinting an amber flash before it darted away, vanishing into the shadows of the hill, seeming to run towards the adobe below.

Strange.

He knew coyotes and wolves weren't that dangerous and normally would avoid people at all costs. Maybe this one was rabid? Or tame? His grip tightened on his gun. Another howl came from his left and then another cry responded somewhere off in the distance. Now those had to be wolves. They were calling to one another. He looked back at the adobe. He shone his flashlight down and could see a worn and rugged path twisting away into the dark.

 Maybe someone is living there. Maybe the damned old woman and her stupid kid.

He had a gun. He'd be fine.

He began to walk down.

*   *   *

He made it down to the clearing without having to stop. He began to walk to the structure, passing by more rocks that reached up out of the earth, black paintings decorating their crimson stone surfaces.

Petroglyphs.

 He walked by them and looked. Most he couldn't identify. They didn't look human. The arms were too long, the heads were warped and unlike any person he'd ever seen. His eyes fell on one that looked familiar. It was a wolf or maybe a coyote. It was huge compared to the humans that sat near it, its eyes looking forward. The people appeared to be worshipping it. The hair on his neck stood.

There are laws older than human laws, John.

 The hitchhiker's voice came back to him.

Fucking ridiculous.

He started to walk quicker, purposely turning his head so as not to look at the black painted figures anymore. He was scared, though he wouldn't admit it. The whole place creeped him out and the petroglyphs made it worse. He could feel their old stone eyes watching him as he walked by.

Outsider

That asshole had called him an outsider. Him! Anger flashed up again. He used it to beat back the fear threatening to consume him. That hitchhiker, he'd find him and teach him a lesson. He forced himself to walk straighter despite the headache now threatening to spill over and force him to rest again.

He arrived at the side of the adobe. Now that he was closer, he could now see a few rusted out and broken cars were scattered about the area. Most had been eaten by the earth, their bodies so rusted he at first didn't know what they were. They were slowly returning to the soil they'd come from. Everything did. A makeshift clothing line hung, strung up between one of the dead cars and an iron rod. A few pieces of what might have been clothes long ago swung in the wind.

The scene made him think of his grandmother and her stories about the Land of the Dead.

"Listen to me, child. Being an unbeliever is almost as bad as being a murderer but not quite, so God sends them there to a place full of dust. It is a dark place. There's no sun, just shadows." She'd look at him in the eyes then and say in a barely audible whisper, *"Believe in our Lord Jesus Christ, child. You'd better believe, or you will end up there, too."*

He shivered at the memory, seeing himself as a child, his tiny hands praying, proving that he believed in Jesus. He'd pray each night like that in hopes that his Grandmother's cruel God wouldn't punish him and send him into the dark like all the unbelievers of the world. He reached up and nervously fingered the cross laying on a small chain around his sunburned neck.

A flash caught his attention, breaking him from his thoughts. A bit of golden light flickered on and then off onto the desert sand in front of him. It was coming from inside the adobe. He turned and now could see the place had a small hole where ruined rag hung like a spider's web. The wind fluttered the rag about, rips and tears letting the light from within creep out with each gust only to be blackened again when the rag fell back. He raised his gun and used it to guide him as he walked up to the small hole to look inside.

At first, no one seemed to be there. In fact, it was devoid of much of anything. There was only a small table fashioned out of an old wooden crate. At the center sat a single half used candle that flickered back and forth in the breeze, painting long shadows on the barren red earth walls.

The dizziness hit again, and he tilted into the clay wall. His head swam so terribly this time that he had to hold himself there to keep from passing out.

Maybe he should have stayed with the car.

A noise from inside snapped him back to reality. It sounded like a woman whispering. He forced himself to look again, angling himself differently. Now he could see who was inside. It was the old Mexican woman he'd seen by the car. He'd found her. He moved back to get ready to confront her by heading through the door off to the side when he heard another voice, a lower gruffer one. He couldn't make out what it was saying. It sounded distorted, slower than it should, and more guttural and the words it spoke,

Are they even words?

He leaned back again and peered in. The old woman was still seated cross legged by the crate and staring at the candle, but now he could see that someone was sitting across from her, the shadow flickering on the floor alongside the old bruja's. She continued talking and finally he picked up one of her words.

"Gringo."

He knew she was talking about him. More guttural noises came, and a bad feeling began to grow in him. Something about this whole situation felt wrong. It was too fucking weird, too surreal. It felt supernatural. He thought again of the petroglyphs and the weird black things with abnormally long arms, the coyote sitting in the center of the worshipping humans.

Suddenly he realized he hadn't even left a note of where he was going on the truck. No one would know where he'd gone. If someone found his truck, would they even know where to look for him? What the hell had he been thinking?

Inside the adobe, the conversation ended signaled by a sudden cessation of noise. He peered in and could see whoever had been seated across from the old woman must have stood as the owner's shadow was stretching across the tiny room's floor like an oil stain, crawling up the other wall, and completely covering the tiny woman in darkness.

Go back to the truck. Fuck this...

Suddenly a face appeared at the window. It wasn't human.

John ran.

Something howled. He turned back to look at the adobe and something black darted out of the structure. It was running towards him. Fast. He picked his legs up trying to run faster, but his damaged body wouldn't allow it. The shape sped through the darkness as other shapes joined it, coming out of the rocks and off the rise off to his right. He felt like he was going to cry. His own weakness disgusted him, and the anger returned. Why was he running? He had the gun.

But what was that, John? What was that in the adobe? What the fuck was that?

I've got a fucking concussion. I'm not thinking right. He snapped back at the internal voice. He wouldn't be treated like this. He was the law.

He stopped running and shouted,

"I've got a gun, you fucking Wetbacks!" he yelled into the darkness. It should have felt powerful but instead it was like yelling down the darkness of an old well. The sound seemed swallowed by the night. A flash of the face came back to him again. The yellow eyes, the asymmetrical mouth full of sharp teeth, the black smoke that seemed to come from it like it was on fire. It had stared at him. One of the shapes suddenly rushed at him and he pulled the trigger. But despite the power of the weapon, he didn't hit it. The thing just swept back and away from him, not even slowing down.

Without warning, something from above was on him, scratching and clawing. It was a bird, a fucking vulture!

 He tried to tear at it, pulling at the feathers and head, but another one appeared. He started batting them away, finally managing to free himself. He began to shoot wildly, hearing himself roaring with fear and anger though the night was still motionless and quiet.

Another whoosh went by him, this time knocking him off his feet. He went sprawling onto the ground, hitting his head again so hard he couldn't breathe for a minute, his gun going off one last time. Darkness began to come over him and he realized he'd shot himself. He almost began to laugh. And just before he went under for the last time, he looked up. Far above he could see a black shape flying. It came spiraling down and down, finally landing near to where he lay. He tried to speak, but he couldn't as the crow watched him with black marble eyes.

Somewhere a wolf began to howl. The coyotes soon joined in.

About the author

Sarah Walker

Sarah Walker is an artist, writer and professor of anthropology and biology at California State University. Her writing has been published by Audient Void, Caravans Awry, Lovecraft E-zine Books, Antimony and Old Lace, Test Patterns, Shoggoth.net, Planet X publications, and more. She is currently at work on her first novel and is also completing finishing touches on her first book of short stories.

She has multiple stories set to be published in 2020 including one set to be published in The Nightside Codex.

Her illustrations have been published by Lovecraft Asylum, Audient Void, Caravans Awry, Test Patterns, and she is currently at work on an illustrated Children's story. Lastly, she is also part of an upcoming comic on the current border situation called *BorderX* in which all money will be donated to The South Texas Human Rights Center.

Sarah spends her free time reading, hiking and hanging out with her partner, many cats, and a large drooling pitbull named Chunky Monkey.

She is an avid Human Rights advocate.

"That just shows when you get good ratings,

you can say anything."

Donald Trump - 2018

Rêves des Cyberdieux: A Nation in Three Acts

By: Maxwell I. Gold

Act 1

They Made Us Great Again: Pour la Patrie

I watched with a beguiling sense of dread as the new gods consumed everything, teasing us with false gifts of innovation and science, cleansing the great Colonial City and poisoning our synapses with gold and blood, unable to go back to a time before.

Inside an awful pantheon near the center of the city, the powdery white deities sat together at a marble slab, graciously decorated with diverse offerings that beautifully echoed the makeup of our nation. Like carrion beasts, only worried about their primal cosmic hunger, they ate and fed, and hoarded every last helping for themselves as the mad god, Ad'Naigon watched with ancient jovial pride, seeing Its pathetic sycophants feed for the sake of Its mercy.

The fat things, whose bugling folds oozed with corn syrupy dreams and fast food slime, engorged themselves with immensities of power and self-indulgence. Coating themselves in the sludge of corporate welfare and shelled falsehoods; their frail carapaces served as a crackling homunculus, leaking misinformation and propagandist trolls gliding through the greyspaces and face-ethers of reality.

"Make it great!" their anthem said, as membranous lips spewed it again and again. The nation saw those brave new words, with a populist fervor that hypnotized our sane dreams. From their Cyclopean capitol in that colonial city, at that harrowed table, they committed their misanthropy; but quelling the noise and detestable shouts that ruptured the spaces above.

On the streets, under black hungering skies, the mobs swarmed over the red bricks with blissful passion as the anger seethed in their eyes. Over the air and through the profuse radioactivity, orange twittered rhetoric polluted the lugubrious forums and online temples with a corrupt palpable sense of mockery. Those once hallowed institutions, now rotting, which for centuries had seemed the most imperious bastions of justice, began to wither from the relentless populism that gnawed at their ivory feet. I felt disgust as I saw them flooding streets. There was nothing else to do but watch as the masses clamored against the high walls of the domed building, its ramparts stretching along the once flowery boulevards bathed in electric light.

The old translucent lamps shimmered gruesomely as the hordes began to sing in dissonant tones outside the gates, where I stood from the balcony's edge with a scornful look. I only thought of the fat and grotesque oligarchs, filled with such paranoia concealed in their alabaster fortress, ignoring the scandalous miasma that permeated the air coiling around the rest of us.

Through instruments of cyanide and silence, we had succumbed to the will of faux statesmen, classless, and weak; plastic gods who manipulated toy men as their puppets and mannequins. Still they fed and fed and fed until nothing remained, but they had made us great, once again.

Act 2

House Un-American

In the empty galleries of those ivory houses on the white hill, silent and grave, gavels slammed with cosmic indifference while dusty orators chortled upending the sovereignty of a generation unborn. Their faces were bleak, pale and cold as if the very light had been drained like a viscous substance to feed some unholy host. These powdery frail creatures were the knights of the dark orange king. They acted only in the nature of his impish will, serving his political expediency, which was their sword, drenched in a yellow fire that would plant itself into the heart of a nation.

Using rusted lances hewn together by iron rhetoric and scorched earth tactics, the world would be singed down to its foundations with no hope of recovery, leaving even the ashes as charred. Into the horizon they went, where Cyber Things twitched like gnats under the guise of some awful god, glimmering with neon eyes. They laughed at the plight of the world, knowing all too well their victory was at hand, cackling in broken phrases and fragmented bytes of *what-ifs* mixed together with *what will never be*!

The Orange King jeered, hailing his servile knights while a generation perished under the silence and convenience of the meager bystanders who simply waited, and watched for something that would never come. In the mist above concealed in his palace of nylon bones and fast food dreams, the fat thing stood happily as copious amounts of amber protoplasm dripped from his neck; the globulous substance a horrid gift from that which was most unfathomable. Dressed in robes of blood and tears, the Revenant Judge took an oath not to a nation, but to himself and to a singular denial of truth.

In the decades to come, nothing remained, except a resentment that continued to fester in the deepest molten pits of a dying land. Like some unnatural blight, spreading from the white hills where those ivory houses stood, his insipid laughter carried over the skies infecting every pitiful soul, drawing them deeper into a state of poisonous hatred. The slime crept through the stars, spilling onto the streets though the people were unmoved, unaware of the evil that coated their skin soaking into their very minds.

We've left nothing for you, no nation in which you have a voice to speak, and for that. . . I'm sorry. How did it really come to this? I thought, sitting there in my room, one of the new tenement homes for royal un-wanteds. Ratty and decrepit, I sat surrounded by posters of resistance and hope, though that's all they'd ever be in this of all houses. A house, un-American.

Act 3

Le Boulevard de Trumpland

And I heard them say, with pustule bliss dripping from their lips, *"Duci decorum est pro patria mori."* That dissonant noise erupted like some unholy choir, filling my ears with an awful black bile. Around the boulevard, where pillars of gold and ivory stood like bastions of a new age, I watched as people were siphoned towards the palatial middle, like ants scavenging for scraps.

It seemed that there was no end in sight. A society consumed by pitiless assaults on self-worth, eating its own morals for the sake of some mythological rusty populism. From the depths of my blue sorrows, wrenched by the fingers of a faceless monster, oceans of ink and plastic flowed from my consciousness as the skies congealed in thick waves of grey windy particulates.

Still, around the boulevard the maggots crawled under neon lights which crackled with an oppressive beat after each flash, each burning pulse. Bright incandescent signs proudly displayed their veneration to a new kind of material god. Encapsulated from reality and hidden from the horrors of the truly dying, decorated in the phosphorescent light of stardust as night fell on the modern streets; these were temples built around the boulevard.

Despite falling skies, yellow eyes were dripping with spectral tears, reactionary fear was their companion and hope was something they abandoned long ago when around the boulevard there was nothing but time and darkness.

The ignorant masses were amongst those who walked the boulevard disregarding indifference as an incompatibility to their own thoughts, an inability which had shown a will to power. In their contemptable ignorance, too late they understood, the nature of humanities limitless follies.

Yet, around the boulevard as the sky grew darker and the neon lights went dim, the people realized it was him who took their world of glittering gems into the most disgusting of places where it would cast a horrid shadow on their once proud faces.

Though he had never seen such temples or boulevards, from the darkness like time he stalked them, waiting in the dank and decrepit swathes of immeasurable horrors. And through the tumult, muck, and grime that terrible orange thing trumped the ground with its flabby gut and rancorous tenor, but the world made not a sound as he stepped out of the ancient dark. His name they'd never speak, despite the misdeeds he'd commit and the holocaust of thought he would spill onto the world.

The stars wept, yet they saw no one walk around that boulevard again, as the skies were clogged even more with a congested soot of brimstone and rancor that plumed so high, reaching the molten pinnacles in that black verdant emptiness above.

And I heard them say, with pustule bliss dripping from their lips, *"Duci decorum est pro patria mori."* Where around the boulevard I walked, alone staring at the empty streets and dead neon signs. I saw a place saturated in the copper flames of liberty and unabated pleasures. The *free world* laid bare before me, for *my* dark leisure.

Neon signs, dancing cable-man marionettes, and puppet gods in white robes devoted to me where in the end I knew I would be free to unleash a hellish woe unlike any other that would make the stars themselves shutter in their heavenly vaults crying molten nuclear tears. The world was on fire, burning with nightmares and obscured realities as wild pyschopomps danced maddeningly in the streets. The end of an empire was near, recalling its outposts from the far reaches of reality while hordes closed in on its cities.

I walked along the broken steps of white mansions and fallen monuments, crumbling at my feet and was beholden to a wondrous sight; my world now covered dust and ruined light. I outlived the hours and times that ticked, away they fell like words and rhetoric through my lips. Once more around the boulevard I walked where no more, no more, would my people live free in this world destroyed, destroyed by me.

About the author

Maxwell I. Gold

Maxwell I. Gold is an author of weird fiction and dark fantasy, writing short stories and prose that primarily center around his cosmic and profane Cyber Gods Mythos. Maxwell's work has appeared in numerous publications including the award-winning literary journal for weird poetry SPECTRAL REALMS, edited by renowned Lovecraft scholar S.T. Joshi, WEIRDBOOK MAGAZINE, THE AUDIENT VOID, HINNOM MAGAZINE from Gehenna and Hinnom Books, as well as SPACE AND TIME MAGAZINE.

He plans to release his debut novella *A Dream of Falling Skies* from Hybrid Sequence Media later this year.

Maxwell studied philosophy and political science at the University of Toledo and currently resides in Columbus, Ohio.

"He's not a war hero.

He's a war hero because he was captured.

I like people that weren't captured."

Donald Trump – 2015

The Tragic Reanimation of Captain John Flag – *A Satire*

By: Scott J. Couturier

The Voice of Reason said it first.

"Ladies and gentlemen, my fellow countrymen, it is my sad duty to inform you that the Wigana virus, a dangerous hemorrhagic pathogen from South America, has crossed our borders and has been reported in the both Texas and Arizona. So far it is limited to the underbreeds, but we suspect it will shortly spread to the White American genome. It grieves me to inform you of this, but rest assured that the Holy Government is currently engaged in a wholesale wipe-out operation. Entire infected villages have been scoured off the map by precision strike-tech, and the borders have been closed and reinforced. We must *not* allow this filth, this foreign contamination, to seep into our cells and infect our children! I stand by the president and the Council of Twelve in supporting these acts of cleansing, may God have mercy on the sub-human souls of the underbreeds."

After this acknowledgment the whole country went to the dogs. The news spread like wildfire, much faster than the plague, though that followed the news in due course. Images flickered on screens across the nation: bloated rotting bodies lying strewn on streets and hanging from windows, black pus streaming from their orifices. Huge machines were brought in to move the bodies, anti-grav military containment vehicles that made no contact with the infected flesh but used modulated soundwaves to shove them towards their common grave. Despite this the disease spread steadily across the country, just as it had spread over the rest of the world, and always the Voice of Reason making declamations, speaking words that immediately became truth:

"The poor are to blame. The poor and their unsanitary living conditions. How, one might ask, does a plague begin? It begins in the cesspit and creeps out. It infects the rest of the world, turns it gray, turns it squalid. You've all heard of rats in the middle ages, rats nipping at the flesh of peasants, who in turn carried the contagion into the most august chambers of church and government. The poor are to blame! The people, the True People, must do away with the diseased limbs of our culture. It is time for John Galt to extricate himself!"

Various Moral Majorities immediately materialized, long planted in the woodwork. The People In Charge had been waiting for a catastrophe, had been on their knees praying for a catastrophe for the last twenty years. Catastrophe drew attention away from the decaying infrastructure, the utterly naked corruption, the daily horrors twisted into virtues by the various ministries of Truth. The True People rose, white skin glistening, and constructed barricades across much of the Midwest. The Wigana virus was halted, at least for the time being; the talk shows entertained a rotating cast of corporate scientists, each one told to feed particular alarming information to the public. Thus, panic endured even after the virus burned out – barely had the final crematory fires extinguished before a closed-border policy was put in place. No citizen of the Imperium of North America could leave the country, and no outsider could enter. It was the beginning of the great Sealing Off.

The poor were exterminated. This posed a daunting challenge, since the unclean hordes had grown so vast in proportion, but thankfully contemporary military hardware was up to the task. The televisions showed little of the butcheries, the miles and miles of casually heaped corpses, the endless screams of children as their parents were taken away for slaughter. Within five years the operation was complete, the Imperium cleansed of 40% of its population. The various Corporate Heads held a parade celebrating the event, with floats and massive balloons representing the symbols of their terrestrial power. All, finally, was settled.

Except that without the poor the very rich had no one to blame for the world's continuing degeneracy. Resources dwindled. Products were designed to be ever-more-defective, and eventually the dumb populace, the stupid gawping populace that had given its blessing to the slaughter of millions, noticed.

But that is another story.

Let us return to the building of the great plague-walls. Smell the rushing concrete, hear the hum and shudder of vast machines, see the sky hidden away behind massive antiseptic tarps. In the midst of these excavations, these desperate works to stave off a rampaging microbe, a chamber was broken into beneath the cyclopean towers of ruined Detro'it, near the shore of Lake Huron (long a seething cauldron of micro-plastics and industrial waste). The unfortunate worker who found the chamber tumbled into it, falling to his death. His fellow workers soon descended on ropes to retrieve the body and investigate the cavern. What they discovered was destined to drastically impact the world's weary turning.

It was a man, suspended in a copper-banded tank hooked to a brass circulating pump. The mechanism was ancient, made of corroded glass tubing and Atlantean pneumatics. The man inside, it was quickly discovered, was still alive, his chest rising and falling in a slow, even pattern, inhaling and exhaling the transparent suspension fluid. Confounded, the workmen raised his stasis-chamber into the light, where it was quickly whisked away by private jet to a subterranean laboratory located somewhere in Maine. There the man's sustaining coffin was unloaded. He was put under surveillance by a team of corpro-military scientists, who quickly arrived at a baffling but unmistakable conclusion: the man in the machine was none other than Captain John Flag.

Captain John Flag. Civil war hero, born and raised in Chicago, known as Grant's Red Right Hand. Thought to be dead for centuries. Yet here, breathing, alive, sealed in a copper-banded glass cocoon. Captain John Flag, Abraham Lincoln's personal bodyguard the night he was shot by that state-certified Demon, John Wilkes Booth.

It was far too much to leak to the state-sanctioned press.

Clearly Captain John Flag had been involved in some covert program to develop a race of supermen. It was revealed, by a team of military arcanists, that following Lincoln's assassination John Flag had gone mad with grief and offered his body and soul as raw material for a shady occult organization known as the Fist of Daedalus. It was thought he had died on the black altar: but now, it seemed, history had returned to haunt the present. Captain John Flag was alive. They had to wake him.

*   *   *

"You, sir, are a genuine American hero," crowed General Radium. Reaching out, he pumped John Flag's hugely muscular arm.

John Flag blinked, pursing his lips. "Am I, sir?"

"That's what the history books say, which is all the truth anyone cares about. How they treatin' you in here, anyways? Looks like a nice room, but are you wanting for anything? Booze? Drugs? Women? Men? I've got some great cocksuckers in my unit downstairs. Not fags, you understand, but good at their job."

John Flag's eyes narrowed in confusion. "No, sir. I just – I don't quite understand where I am."

"Where you are? Why m'boy, you're at the crossroads of American history! Or rather, I guess you *are* the crossroads of American history." General Radium began pacing the small, clean, LED-lit room, a fuming Cuban eCigar clenched between his mottled lips. "Tell me, boy, what can you remember? For crissakes, you knew old Honest Abe! You've got to tell me, what was he like?"

John Flag licked at his lips, still chapped as a result of his stasis. "Tall," he said.

"Of course he was! And what about that Civil War, huh? Musta been good fun, fightin' off those Graybacks. The stench of gunpowder, the screams of the wounded, oh –" here General Radium reached down to clutch at his groin, which was swelling visibly. "Sorry about that, m'boy. Seem to have got myself into a state of arousal. Why don't you just tell me what you can remember, and I'll listen, eh? And don't skimp on the good stuff."

Captain John Flag obeyed. After all, this was clearly a superior officer. He told what he could remember about his childhood and adolescence, talked about the war, talked about the few conversations he could remember with president Lincoln. Most of it was vague, lost in a gray-black haze. At the last he talked about his association with the Fist of Daedalus, which he remembered in far more piercing detail.

"They chained spirits in me," he said, raising and flexing his massive arms. "I don't know how else to describe it, sir. There was a chemical process – lots of needles and tubes – and chanting, hours and hours of chanting. But the real source of my power comes from a world beyond our senses. Seeing they had created a monstrosity, the order decided to freeze me, put me away and use me as a template for studying their mistakes." John Flag sniffed, rose from the edge of his linen-draped bed and approached General Radium, who was listening with a disconcerting glint in his right eye. "Sir, I've told you everything I know. Now I ask you to return the favor. What year is this? Why have I been brought out of hibernation now?"

General Radium laughed, reached up and clapped a clammy hand on John Flag's perfectly sculpted shoulder. "Good questions, my boy, good questions. It was mighty nice of you to tell me all that, though it seems your mind's gone a little patchy."

John Flag nodded. "Yes sir. There are many things I should remember, but they're just...not there."

"Yes, yes. Probably for the best." The general snickered as he crossed to a window tinted so heavily as to appear black. "You want to know when this is? My boy, what's time good for but as a means of getting from here to there?" Reaching out, he touched a hand to the umbra-black glass. Immediately the window became clear. Undiluted sunlight blasted inwards, but John Flag's modified body responded in stride, his pupils contracting without so much as a wince. He stepped forward, staggered, and reeled in awe at the sight before him.

It was a city. A thoroughly modern city, sculpted of plasteel and various recycled substances, tall gray fume-spewing towers stabbing up towards skies rendered perpetually purple by the Great Chemical Disaster of 2103. John Flag's eyes widened, and he raised his massive hands and pressed them to the glass, against which his breath was pooling and dissolving.

"What is this place?" he demanded, feeling unsteady, as if the floor could no longer support his weight.

General Radium smiled. "Why, it's Earth, m'boy! Good old Mother Earth, the bitch, with just a few modifications and makeovers. And not only is it Earth, but it's America, the land you fought for, the land your legend helped create!"

John Flag closed his eyes for a moment, then opened them wide, taking in the hideously alien vista. He trembled and turned away. "What year is it?" he asked dully, eyes boring into the equally alien plastic-coated floor.

"2239," the general said. He emitted a puff of tobacco-scented vapor, drew out the eCigar and ritualistically tapped it against the windowsill. "AD, of course, though the atheist academic faggots had their go at stripping Christ out of history. Thankfully they've all been wiped out, by the grace of our Lord and Savior."

John Flag frowned. "Faggots? Do you mean bundles of wood?"

"Jesus son, no! I mean the born cocksuckers, the jizz-guzzlers, the Brothers of the Gaping Stinkhole!" The general became flustered and started pacing, his bloodshot eyes darting around the room like agitated flies. He paused, inhaling a snort of powder from a plasteel pyx. "Hm. You're behind, boy, dangerously behind. If you're gonna rally the people and exemplify the greatness of this country you're gonna need some schooling, that much is clear."

"Rally the people?" John Flag felt a sour sensation blossom in his stomach, but he ignored it. America still existed, even in 2239; if he could ensure its continued existence it was his duty to do so, regardless of personal cost or bewilderment. "Sir, are the people in need of rallying? What is the political situation in this day and age?"

General Radium guffawed. "It's whatever we want it to be," he said with a wink and a snort. Reaching into his pocket he pulled out a slim pamphlet and pressed it into John Flag's colossal right hand. "Take a look at that. Should explain most of it."

John Flag opened the pamphlet, amazed at the glossy sheen and texture of the paper. *REPUBLICRATS AND DEMOCRANS,* read the heading. This was underlined by a smaller clump of text, written boldly: *It is every citizen's responsibility to feel fear and unreasoning hatred.*

John Flag furrowed his magnificent antediluvian brow. "I don't understand."

"Well of course not, son. You've got to read the whole thing."

The supersoldier frowned further and continued reading. *Join one of our two approved political parties and fulfill your national duty by fiercely disagreeing with everything done by the opposing party! This maintains the Generative Dichotomy of American politics, which has made us the driving force in the industry of modern warfare. All around the country men and women are busy constructing bombs, building laser carbines, putting the final spit-and-polish on the noses of sub-orbital death shuttles! Support the troops, support the strength of the American dollar, support the next war. And, ABOVE ALL support the political party of your choice and oppose the political party not of your choosing. Remember, you are completely right and those who think differently are completely wrong. Don't forget to vote!*

John Flag handed the pamphlet back feeling thoroughly and menacingly confused. "I still don't understand," he said, a ripple of apprehension running through his exquisite sinews.

The general crumpled up the pamphlet and threw it into a corner. "Forget it. All you need to know is that America is wavering. What the old girl needs is a hero, a true hero, from a more gilded and honorable age. Me and the higher brass think you're just the antique for the job."

Antique? Like everything from his time, from rusted plows to cracked china to books smelling of centennial mold to bayonets long-dry of blood (unbeknownst to him all remaining Civil War bayonets had long been repurposed as sacrificial daggers). Captain John Flag hunkered down within himself, trying to focus the dimness of his inner vision.

General Radium wrapped a flab-heavy arm halfway around John Flag's titanic shoulders. "Trust me, boy. You're gonna be the toast of the free world. Tours, interviews, television spots, the works. The Voice of Reason is already standing by to announce your resuscitation!"

John Flag blinked, his quest to seek out solidity in his amorphous soul coming to naught. "The Voice of Reason?" he parroted with little genuine curiosity.

"Oh, yes. John Ribbles Plunker, the Truest American, though he might have to turn that title over to you. He keeps the

Republicrats and Democrans properly riled up and pushes the corporate war agenda via outraged moral justifications and hysterical humanism. Wonderful chap. We've got you an interview scheduled on his show next week." The general chuckled and reached for the knob on a paper-thin radio. Immediately a bold, assured, potent voice burst from microscopic speakers, beamed down from the firmament by unerring satellites:

"And now the New Poor, as they call themselves, are coming to Washington DC begging for handouts! Am I the only one who realizes that we just took care of this problem? What's next, people marrying themselves or demanding commie health care? It's all a slippery slope, a slippery slope, which is why I say firmly and in the knowledge of my complete rightness: get over it. The American Dream is just a dream until you wake up and do something about it. Pick yourselves up by your bootstraps, and if you can't afford boots get a job, buy a pair, and start tugging. This isn't a nation of freeloaders, a truth reflected in our recent extermination policies. Now, speaking of freeloaders, the recently acquired Canadian territories are complaining AGAIN about injustices carried out by our stalwart occupying forces. This is base slander, and as I said in my recent book –"

Captain John Flag's eyes glossed over as he listened to the charismatic ramblings of the hallowed Voice of Reason. General Radium, content that his task was accomplished, left the room, teeth grinding on the stem of his perpetually smoldering eCigar.

*   *   *

The tendency of moths to hurtle headlong into flame has been oft remarked upon. There is a joy in their self-demise, an awareness of mortal danger trumped by the need for ecstatic experience. So potent is the moth's relationship to its own self-imposed fiery demise that it has become a living metaphor, signifying both foolishness and transmutation. Human mocks Moth for its self-immolating ways, yet somehow feels a sense of vicarious union, possibly even *jealousy*, and cannot help but imagine the sheer joy of death-by-divine-fire.

Of course, it's generally the way of Human to perceive their own interpretation of the Universe as the highest and most evolved. How could it be otherwise? Look at the wonders that spill forth from Mankind's making hands! Machines to accomplish every task, to reshape reality and allow ever-upwards rocketing of populations, to lengthen life while shearing away the enjoyments of the flesh, to PROLONG AND EXTEND until the diseased and neglected framework of social mechanism finally collapses, unsubtly burying Humanity in the ruin of their most exquisite subtleties. How could this not be the ultimate pinnacle of evolved consciousness?

And yet Human, this being of multiply layered brains, has one stark defect, which is the everlasting source of their self-horror: they die. They die and leave behind a sack of rotting matter, still sculpted in the semblance of self but rapidly fading, preservable only through expedited means of mummification. This whole state of affairs terrifies Human: they spend all their living breathing blood-pumping days dwelling in the inevitable shadow of the grave. It hinders them, and spurs them on, and ultimately (save in cases of certain mystics whose hearts burn with the intensity of an ember for days after their deaths, whose terminal exhalation is a sigh of compassionate relief) forces them to die afraid, fearing oblivion or hellfire or a thousand other metaphysical fates. Or, alternatively, nonbeing.

This brings us, by logical degrees, back to the humble flame-revering moth. Patience, not-so-gentle reader. All will finally be revealed.

Human is in the habit of laughing at the apparent stupidity of the moth. This tendency has declined somewhat with the invention of the electric light, which the moth can dance around eternally without the satisfaction of immolation, but still Human laughs at the dumbly hurtling things, boinging endlessly off luminous glass carapaces. Human wonders why the moth cares so little for its life when they care for the preservation of their own so immensely; inevitably they conclude the moth is just plain stupid. In truth (here is the grand secret) Human is far less evolved than the humble death-embracing moth. The moth understands implicitly that its current incarnation, that of a small fluttering powder-winged insect, is designed by nature to perish. It occupies a stratum of life that is consumed by other stratum of life. Yet, the moth also understands (better than all its crawling brethren) the passionate lure of the divine light, and so hurls itself without thought or care into the crucible of its own death and remaking. In this way the moth is evolved far beyond the petty perceptions of Human, who eyes death with crisis-inducing unease and considers the descent of its scythe a bane and a horror.

When a human dies they become a swarm of moths, if they be so privileged as to matriculate upwards.

Now, harsh and unforgiving reader, let's guide this whole straggling train of thought back to our ferociously patriotic hero. Captain John Flag, a man of power and will, yet also a man of limited self-determination, a man designed to bend to and accomplish the designs of others. He is an Aries with Pisces rising and a Pisces moon, a perpetual smoldering fire whose production of steam could power a late-Victorian empire, yet he yearns to dedicate this boundless energy to pre-determined causes. He is, as are all beings, at a stage of his ongoing development, and had he died and been properly reborn these oppositional elements of the Self would have transmuted, reordered, and expanded. However, in giving himself over to the dark rituals of the Fist of Daedalus, in allowing himself to be arcanely preserved rather than die at the appointed time (a horse-riding accident at age 59, at approximately 2:37 PM on July 8th 1889), he ceased evolving in his current form and became a creature of unnatural stagnation, an avatar of festering, languishing purpose. His mind, once obsessed with ideals and concepts of justice, a fiery forge wherein metals of various virtue were perpetually smelted and reformed, has become foggy and vague, haunted by his past in the 19th century as a dreamer's mind is haunted upon awakening by disturbing visions. He remembers Abraham Lincoln, but only as a silhouette, a gangling outline with a huge hair-studded mole as its only determining characteristic. He remembers the stink of blood and gunpowder on the battlefield, remembers fighting in the war, the swarms of differently hued jackets plowing into each other with cries of righteous butchery, but all particulars are lost in the miasmic perception of the whole. He is, quite literally, a man without a concrete past, who even as I write this is thumbing through history books questing for the truth of his own legend. He is confused, tetherless, adrift in the 23nd century, knowing only the vague pride of his former self, feeling quite keenly the undying nature of his cells and the potential foggy eternity stretching before him.

The sky is purple. The buildings rise like leviathans into the sky. The breadth of human learning can be summoned to a portable device that fits in one's pocket, can even be installed into one's brain, creating a synthesis of 'actual' and 'virtual' (or 'constructed') reality. Were John Flag a whole man, a dweller of the 19th century suddenly propelled forward via some palpitation of time, he would find such a future unbearably alien. In his now-foggy form, dulled by centuries of slumber, he merely feels odd and out-of-place. His cells, programmed by uncouth medicines and incantations, adapt readily to any environment, and it will not be long before he finds his place and purpose in this new world and soldiers on, quite literally. Not for him the fear of death, for it will never find him save in battle, which is his native purpose. Like the moth speeding towards flame he speeds towards war; his place in Valhalla is assured.

A calming, solidifying, constantly comforting presence in John Flag's new life was the hallowed Voice of Reason. It told him what to think, how to think about it, and what not to think. He learned all about the harnessing of electricity and the Blasphemies of Tesla, learned about the glorious ascendance of the Oil Gods and the Corporate Pantheon. The missing pieces of his past dissipated further, becoming less than shadows, while his present became clotted with the rhetoric of New Patriotism. He learned all about the Wigana virus, which had poured into North America via the veins of the foreign poor; by the time he got to the parts about the mass executions and mountainous communal graves his heart and spirit were already conditioned to regard these atrocities as necessary. He was Captain John Flag, the ultimate soldier, to whom the orders of his superiors defined the perimeters of reality. Within a month he had turned into a stolid, rabid nationalist, had projected much of his new learning into the remembered guise of Abraham Lincoln, the revered American president who had died on his watch. John Flag had a secret talisman, and he rubbed it between his thumb and forefinger often: it was a single follicle of Honest Abe's beard. He fiddled with it unobtrusively during his on-air interviews, laid it out on his bedside table every night, often fell asleep staring at its frayed silhouette. He showed it to John Ribbles Plunker when he appeared on the Voice of Reason's radio show, though the show's host could not be seen, hidden behind a pane of one-way reflective glass. The Voice promised to tell no one, and at the resumption of their interview after the obligatory half-hour of corporate commercial programming he turned over to Captain John Flag the much-revered title of Truest American. They then talked about the new Zamboni ban in the Canadian colonies, briefly discussed the qualities they looked for in the ideal woman (subservient, hairless, sexually obliging, plump), and parted as friends.

Captain John Flag. Celebrity, idol of the state, endorsing various shaving creams and fast-food chains. Captain John Flag, for whom his own past was a legend. Captain John Flag, who blithely declared the upcoming year of 2240 as the Year of the Billy Bang's Combustible Pellet Gun (the current year being the Year of the Napalm-brand Cluster Bomb). The concept of corporate sponsorship for each year had been gleaned from David Foster Wallace's *Infinite Jest*, now considered a national classic alongside the collected oeuvre of Ayn Rand. These books Captain John Flag did not read, but very reliable government officials briefed him on the revelations they contained. Thus, he became a New American.

*   *   *

"I'll admit it still confuses me that Christianity is the state religion, but Bibles are banned."

The shriveled priest waved a dismissive hand, gemstones glittering at the swollen intersections of his joints. "The Bible is far too powerful for the average American to comprehend. Better it be held in custodianship by those with the wisdom to understand and interpret it."

Captain John Flag squirmed on his velvet-cushioned chair. It was five months since his reanimation. He'd starred in three films, endorsed twenty-seven products, had more cash-credits to his name than most of the carefully tended Middle-Upper Class. He had learned to hate, had absorbed the flavor of propaganda like tofu fried between two T-bone steaks (genuine meat, not vat-grown), and perpetually wore a pristine blue-and-white military uniform specially designed to accommodate his muscle-riddled body. He had come to speak to the priest on a matter of faith which had been troubling him the past two months; now his query was answered, quickly and succinctly. The elderly priest blinked and smiled.

"Was that all you had to ask, my son? Or is there another reason for this visit?"

John Flag collapsed back into his massive chair. It was specifically tailored to his size, borne wherever he went by a sycophantic entourage made up of patriots, journalists, veterans, religious fanatics, and state-sponsored paparazzi. Now the velvet grated against his skin like jagged iron.

"Father, I've heard the words of the Voice of Reason. I see why New Nationalism is necessary for the survival of the state. But at the same time, I perceive immense hypocrisy at the highest levels of church and government."

The priest smiled at this, though without mirth. "There is no longer a division, remember."

"Of course. Now, I don't suppose it's any different than the 19th century, corruption being the oldest human invention. But at least in the 19th century people valued truth over lies. Now it's the exact opposite."

The priest's smile turned to a sneer. "Understanding and accepting the corruption of government was necessary for the human race to advance. We spent millennia trying to stamp it out, burning down palaces and beheading the rich, and to what end? Another corrupt institution always rises in the place of the old, sounding the horns of transparency and justice. We're much better off being willingly manipulated, don't you see?"

Captain John Flag nodded slowly, rubbing the fiber of Abraham Lincoln's beard between his right thumb and forefinger. "So hypocrisy is now truth," he muttered.

"Truth is whatever is decided by those in power. So it's always been, but never has it been more open, more freely admitted and embraced." The priest reached for a small bronze bell on his desk and rang it insistently. The door to the rectory office opened to admit a shivering naked boy, his pale eyes glassy and wide-blown. At the priest's mute gesture, he fell on all fours and crawled beneath the cleric's robe. The priest sighed, flexed his body, and cast John Flag a pristine white smile.

"See the benefits? Of course, I have to allow a girl to please me once a week to avoid being accused of homosexuality, but it's a very minor restriction." The priest gasped then, arcing his back, and a furiously blushing John Flag rose and fled the room without another word. Several moments later his entourage entered and bore away the great chair, all throats bent to singing songs of the motherland.

*   *   *

"The Corporation is beyond humanity. It is an amalgamated sentience, a god of innumerable faces, the guise of Osiris and Buddha and Christ and Mohammad wedded to the Great Truth of capitalism. So worship, all ye people! Go and buy the brand that most completely expresses your individual self! Find your niche and fill it gloriously! For God is benevolent yet jealous, His collective eye all-seeing."

Captain John Flag was being ferried to some military to-do in the extreme Alaskan north. He turned off the radio and sighed, casting his eyes down to the endless rotting swampland below. Once this had been tundra, but the Period of Warming had melted the age-old ice, freeing strange paleolithic diseases and opening up new reserves of fossil fuels for extraction. The virulent purple sky had taken some getting used to, but finally he could look out the window of an airplane without feeling contaminated and nauseous. Far more disturbing than the hue of the sky was the swamp, the teeming fetid hungry swamp. Malformed animals chased the plane's shadow across pools of stagnant chemicals, and the stink of the mire was evident even in the cabin's heavily-filtered air.

"Attention," came the pilot's wheezing voice, projected through the overhead. "We are proceeding on schedule. Our current ETA is 6:00 PM Mountain Time. Please enjoy the refreshing chemicals available in your overhead mask, and if you have any needs whatsoever inform the in-flight AI."

John Flag sighed and slid the shutter down, feeling dull and depressed. Absently he reactivated the radio-unit.

"...and here we are at the infamous Panopticon Gallery in New York City, eagerly awaiting the arrival of pop art sensation Timothy Spunk. His latest display of Fart Art will be unveiled to the public this evening, and we have personal assurances from the mayor herself that the keys to the city will be presented to the

once-controversial, now ravishingly popular pioneering artist."
There was a crackle of manufactured static, then an archival
recording of Timothy Spunk began speaking, his voice thin with
youth and strain.

"You know, it takes a visionary to have a vision. So, yeah,
uh. Human flatulence...well, once people thought it was irritating,
right? Or funny. But now...haven't we all heard a corpse or two
empty its bowels? Or had a relative who died from dysentery. It
goes from being funny to ghastly. So I thought, why not take back
the fart, you know? That's what my installation does: the fart as
comedy, the fart examined as a social awkwardness. The fart as
flammable! We come at farts from all angles. But don't worry – the
displays don't smell unless you get the nasal app."

John Flag deactivated the radio. He raised his right ass
cheek and farted, and knew it to be art.

Raising the shutter, he again peered down on the gruesome
chemical swamp teeming with distorted life. To the horizon – the
land turned purple too, blending in with the sky. Something stirred
in him as memories moved from senescence. At last he began to
remember who he was.

The plane landed just as he was starting to really figure
things out.

The ceremony involved the opening of a new, huge oil rig.
Somehow this was deemed to be of strategic national importance.
John Flag waved and smiled. Once, this had all been ice: what
remained was burned away by the deployment of vast mirrors in
outer space. *Outer space*...so much new information. So muddled!
John found himself shaking hands. Hundreds and hundreds of
hands. Smiles, too: bright and white and beautiful. Almost every
hand was slick with something, sweat or – oil?

A thousand balloons were released. The rig started up operations. The polluted water below boiled and churned as oil was sucked up from the ocean's nethers.

John Flag found himself surrounded by crowds of chirruping children, all wanting to hug him or get his autograph. Many of them were waving toys he had endorsed.

One of the toys – a goggle-eyed fuzzy thing called a Snazzle, they had their own morning cartoon show – exploded.

The blast ignited the oil well. Within seconds the entire facility erupted in white-hot flame. A large number of Very Important People were killed, but not John Flag. Nothing so crude as flame could undo his curse. He plummeted into the irradiated Pacific, straight down to the bottom of that soupy mess, where he was gobbled up by a tumorous Fuku-fish.

It took months for John Flag to slog successfully through the leviathan's quadruple-stomach tract. He was excreted the worse for wear, flesh flensed almost to bone by the thing's harsh digestive juices. He washed up on the shore of what was once California: when he came to and staggered inland he saw entire cities leveled by the dreadful Wigana virus. He saw government sprayers – blazoned with the single-star flag of the Imperium – misting down a fine haze of infective spore. He felt his heart – enslaved to new ideas and concepts, hitched to the wheel of a Satanic Mill – thunder in his chest, struggling to keep up the flow of eldritch blood leaking from him in bursts at each step.

"There's only dignity in making others undignified. You want human dignity? Show me a swimming pool, a jet, a yacht, twenty pert broads, a few twinks for flavor. All the coke I can snort. And a good gore-covered battlefield on the monitor to pay for it all...you ever bomb a village while getting a blowjob? That's dignity, my friend. Living it large and living easy. Living off the backs, sweat, and suffering of others – it's what Mother Nature intended. The bitch."

General Radium's voice rattled around inside John's head like a bird trapped in an attic.

He coughed as the Wigana virus coated him, burning his naked nerve endings. He felt virulence flush his body – would the imperfect magics of the Fist of Daedalus serve to sustain him? He remembered endless black days navigating that *thing's* stinking craw...John did something he wasn't supposed to be able to do. He vomited.

The plague rained down, down, doing the will of the Voice of Reason. John Flag spat and started his staggering march towards Washington, intent on reporting for duty.

About the author

Scott J. Couturier

Scott J. Couturier is a writer of the Weird, grotesque, liminal, & darkly fantastic. His poetry & prose began cropping up in literary journals & anthologies in 2017 – venues he has contributed to include *The Audient Void, Spectral Realms, Hinnom Magazine, Space & Time Magazine, & Weirdbook,* while his fiction has been repeatedly featured in the *Test Patterns & Pulps* anthologies from Planet X Publications.

He stands wholeheartedly opposed to fascism's creeping degeneracy.

"I don't even wait. And when you're a star, they let you do it. You can do anything, grab 'em by the pussy. You can do anything."

Donald Trump – 2005

The King, In Orange

By: Duane Pesice

The third impeachment of HIS fourth term was going swimmingly, the RIGHT having gained a voting body after a particularly gruesome betrayal of values.

President Yam screwed his pants on, gathered his phalanx of enablers, tweeted a few syllables, and settled down to watch on tv.

"That's entertainment!" He exclaimed as his handpicked surrogates destroyed the defense with a fusillade of well-placed ad hominems and extraneous garbage.

But the voting was going against him.

One Senator in particular was drumming up opposition.

Yam glowered. "I should have gotten rid of that guy years ago," he groaned. "But we wanted to keep up appearances."
"That's right!" exclaimed the gallery. "You're right!"

"Of course, I Yam," he growled.

Long years before, Yam had bragged that he could shoot someone on Fifth Avenue and get away with it.

"Let's put that to the test," he remarked, and departed for the

Senate's house.

"… years ago, terrorists tried to destroy America. Today, we're showing that we know how to do it ourselves," said Senator Hector to the body politic. "I can't be a party to this."

President Yam said, "meet me on Fifth Avenue," and shot Senator Hector in the head three times, just to be sure.

And the assembled threw off the yoke of the proletariat as a body, voting yea to the reconstituted Constitution.

"Long live the King, in Orange."

"I yam what I yam," The emperor agreed. "I have only the best words, the best thoughts, and the best wishes. Let's get THEM."

And so the Yam Dynasty was born, according to legend. It was a destructive dynasty that was only ended when relatives of Senator Burrow took out Yam's entire family fortune by cornering the guano market, thereby depriving them of their chief commodity.

The Yams declared bankruptcy, and according to their own bylaws, were shot at sunrise, as there was no hope of recompense any longer, meaning that there wasn't a reason to keep them alive.

The former Mrs. Yam narrowed her eyes at their fall, viewing them from the distance of her dacha on the Caspian Sea, where she had been retired after removing the root of Emperor Yam and planting it in the compost heap, where its little button head poked out from the muck and shit.

She sighed happily and enjoyed another moloko, oh my droogies. The dwarves went back to work on her.

"I will miss you, Papa," she said. "Please, a little lower. Oh yes."

Their actions hardly moved her strings.

Her mother watched, inviolate, immaculate. Her orifices had been sewn shut and paved over, and her catlike eyes gleamed in the dusk. She took her brain out and played with it, dropping it once or twice.

"The party comes to you," said a voice from the darkness.

Emperor Yam chortled happily at the fake news of another market record and sipped his diet Coke while chewing his bacon burger. A woman with a vaguely familiar face and titanic breasts serviced him while he ate and tweeted.

The Mrs. had recently taken up whittling. She watched the news and worked away at a vaguely cylindrical object, taking care to sharpen her blade periodically, and also to burnish her nails against the stone.

She was in her room, he in his. There was an adjoining door, but she had secured it with cinder blocks and just a bit of barbed wire. The decorator, who had recommended an electric fence, was nonplussed.

Had.

It was currently as unsecured as his cell phone. She was just waiting for him to discover that.

At length, he did.

He was naked and ready when he came to her in the night. She encouraged his attentions and presently delivered her dark benediction.

"I Yam ready to come!" he hollered. "Get ready!"

She lowered her drawers and gushed forth, emptying her bladder while he writhed in ecstasy, bringing her frame down to rest on his overlarge abdomen.

She carved quickly, before the people who had been shooting the video could interfere.

"Finally!" she exclaimed. "I am rid of him!"

"Not really," said his double, entering the room.

"Not really," said his triple. And so on.

A roomful of Yam.

"But we're bored with this Presidency shit," he said. "There must be new worlds to conquer. I have only the best advisors and I have only the best brain to make the best decisions. I am a stable super-genius."

And they converged on her and bore her away. President Plutkin was eager to help.

"She will have her own special gulag," he said via phone, rubbing his hands together. "Congratulations on the monarchy."

"Thank you," he said, and headed down to the tanning booth, where they painted his skins on and did his combovers.

He made his tv appearance and issued his edicts. Business as usual.

About the author

Duane Pesice

Duane Pesice resides in the desert southwest with his machines and animals. His writings on various subjects have been published in numerous journals and anthologies, and he threatens more on a daily basis.

"You know what they used to do with guys like that

when they were in a place like this?

They'd be carried out on a stretcher folks. Oh, It's

true."

Donald Trump – 2016

Suppress This

By: Paul Blake

"Ladies and gentlemen, I proudly present to you your still, and undefeated, heavyweight president of the United States of America," the announcer proclaimed into the microphone.

Donny T strutted on to the stage from the wings. Out of time with the 'Eye of the Tiger' playing through the many speakers around the New York Hilton Midtown's Grand Ballroom. The site of his 2016 victory. His patented waddle—shuffle—walk was in full effect. Fireworks went off on either side of the stage as he reached the podium. Confetti and balloons fell on the hundreds of donors and sycophants that made up the crowd. All of them sporting this season's must-have nationalist fashion accessory. The red MAGA cap from 2016 had evolved into a Stars and Stripes monstrosity displaying the moniker 'Trump Made America Great Again'.

Trump flapped his hands around in a pitiful attempt at shadow boxing as the music faded. He waved his balloon animal arms to dampen the artificial applause that had been pumped into the room for the watching TV public. Eventually, someone found the button, and it died down. Trump started his speech with his trademark public speaking Adderall sniff and began, "Thank you…

thank you. A huge result. Incredible. It's great to be back here in the Hilton— Classy joint —To celebrate another tremendous victory by me. Millions and millions of hardworking, honest Americans chose me again, instead of that Democrat loser. I won. I beat the fake news lamestream media. I beat that loser. I beat the liberals and the elite. Again." At the end of each sentence, Trump punctuated his speech with jabs of his pudgy forefinger. "They tried everything to defeat me. But I beat them. They'll be at home drinking their tears. We're here celebrating. This time we stopped their electoral fraud as well. That's right. After the last election with the fraudulent 'popular' vote lies. I made sure this wouldn't happen again. Your President swept the board with the Electoral College and a true Popular vote. Really showing those libs what a winner is—"

<Click>

"Dad, why did you turn that off? The President was speaking," Corry asked. He was lying on a beanbag in front of the television.

"It's past one, you've got school in the morning. I just wanted to see if it was true, whether they'd realize they made a mistake. I guess it happened again." His dad sounded broken. Despondent. Slurred. Corry thought the half-empty bottle of liquor on the table might have something to with that.

Corry, like most of the other boys in his sixth-grade class, thought Trump was doing a good job. Standing up for honest Americans. Corry was proud of his country. They were God's chosen, after all. During recess, they played Trump's speeches on their phones. They used words like 'yuge', 'bigley', 'lame', 'winners' sprinkled in their everyday conversation. Corry was looking forward to walking into school in the morning, wearing his TMAGA hat straight and proud and shooting the 's-word' with his friends, pissing off the losers in class.

"Come on. Bed. Brush your teeth."

"Yes, Dad," Corry sighed. He stood up and gave his dad a hug. "Night, Dad."

"Night, Corry. Sleep well."

Corry left the room with a final look back at his dad, catching the tears sliding down his father's face.

Corry's Dad, Jordan Strickler, sat back in his chair and let the tears fall. He'd heard the reports in the weeks before the election. People being purged off the voting register. It happens every election, he'd thought. They can't remove that many, he'd thought. Those people would be able to get back on the register, he'd thought. The integrity of the democratic system couldn't be broken, he'd thought.

He'd thought wrong.

In the run-up to the 2020 Presidential Election, there had been an unprecedented level of purging the voter records. From sixteen million records removed between 2014-2016 to twenty-six million between 2018-2020. All in the name of protecting against voter fraud. That voter fraud is practically non-existent and at best ineffectual was beside the point. The Republican-controlled state legislatures decimated the number of eligible voters. If they can't vote, they can't vote against us.

News reports showed angry demonstrations outside government offices across the country from people struck off and unable to re-register. The legislatures enacted strict removal of voters that did not vote in previous elections and removed millions of voters whose registration did not "exact-match" their government-issued documents. They also increased the strictness of what documents they'd accept towards registration. State IDs were no longer acceptable, only passports, driving licenses issued within that state, military IDs and concealed carry permits were acceptable. Registration centers that were already stretched beyond capacity had their opening hours cut, and many were closed altogether. These measures were designed to remove whole swathes from the voter pool. Poorer and predominantly minority citizens faced an uphill battle trying to get registered. Expensive IDs were way out of the budgets of many Americans already struggling to pay their rent and feed their children. This deliberate disenfranchisement delivered Trump his second term.

Trump's popular vote figure dropped from 62,984,828 in 2016 to 58,324,546 in 2020; however, the Democrat vote was far less than that. From Hillary's almost 66 million votes to 42,525,612. A drop of twenty-eight million voters nationwide from 2016. A triumph for manipulation and underhandedness. A tragedy for democracy and one person one vote.

A few months after the election, Trump was due to visit Lexington, Kentucky. Living in Scottsburg, a two-hour drive away, Corry had been badgering his father to attend the Trump speech from the moment he first heard about it. His friends were doing the same to their parents. Corry offered to give up his allowance to cover the gas and do extra chores for the chance to see the President. Too young to be registered a Young Republican, he had started a Trump Youth movement at his school that had spread to surrounding districts. The movement had made local media coverage with the school's principal saying what an example the children had set to the rest of the school. Discipline had improved, as well as attendance. The Trump Youth accepted children from the age of ten. Corry had persuaded some of his friend's parents to accompany the movement on hikes and campouts. At these events, the children read excerpts of Trump's speeches, sang songs around the campfires and practiced weapons training. Corry's father never attended, much to Corry's shame.

The day before the visit, Jordan relented. He figured Corry would get one of the other parents to take him. He'd rather be there with Corry and refute each one of the Commander-in-Chief's lies as they flew out his mouth. By seeing Trump live and in person, as the deceitful, criminal scumbag he was, Jordan thought it'd break Corry from the monster's hypnotic spell. He had to try, right?

They left for the rally the next morning. Corry wearing a t-shirt featuring Trump wearing the WWE Championship belt and the slogan 'The Greatest', and his Star-Spangled Banner TMAGA baseball cap. Jordan wore a blue shirt and jeans. The rally wasn't due to start until seven that evening, but Jordan had heard security was tight at these events, so they got there early. They arrived at the Rupp Arena, joined the line that already stretched past the Lexington Center, the Hyatt Regency, and onto the junction with South Broadway. As far as Jordan could tell he was the only one there not wearing the flag in some form or another.

When they finally got into the arena, there was still an hour to go before the rally was to start. They were led to their seats in the bleachers. A sea of red, white, and blue between them and the stage. An ocean of the same behind them. Jordan could see a line of tan brown-shirted security at the edge of the stage. Looking like the picture's he'd seen of the Hell's Angels at the Altamont Free Concert in the Sixties. I wouldn't want to mess with them, Jordan thought. The stage itself was adorned with the Stars and Stripes, hundreds of them covering the floor. At the back of the stage, behind the podium were a few rows of supporters. From Jordan's position, they all looked relatively young, good-looking, and white, of course.

A minute or so before the event, an excited hush spread across the crowd. Everyone looked towards the stage and waited. And waited. From the back of the stage, supporters started chanting, "Trump! Trump! Trump!" This was picked up on by the rest of the crowd. Still, no Trump. The call didn't die down. Jordan thought it was getting louder. People started stomping with every 'Trump'. Jordan looked at Corry. The boy's eyes were sparkling, and he had a wide grin on his face as he joined in with the crowd.

Trump eventually entered the stage from the side. The crowd exploded with noise. He waved at the crowd and walked out to the podium. As he crossed the stage, Jordan thought, he is literally stepping on the flag, and these guys are loving it. Trump waved his arms for the cheers to subside, then appeared to change his mind and gestured for them to up the volume. The crowd responded to their puppet master. After a few minutes, it stopped, and Trump began his speech. He held the crowd spellbound. They finished his sentences. They booed on cue. They laughed when he did.

With every lie or mistruth from the president, Jordan tried giving Corry the truth, the facts, but he was soon overwhelmed by the number of falsehoods coming from the stage. Before he had even started to refute one, another would take its place. Eventually, he gave up and watched with a rising level of disgust. He had never watched a full Trump speech before. Clips shared on Facebook didn't capture the sheer level of bullshit from the man. He wasn't a great orator. He picked topics seemingly at random as they occurred to him, veering off the subject into wild tangents and conspiracies, but the crowd loved him.

Jordan's anger grew with each fiction.

Trump started talking about how the election was a triumph for democracy, how he won with the biggest majority in history, how he was the most popular president of all time. When Trump said, he was looking to become the 'longest runningest' president by changing the twenty-second amendment which says a person can only be elected to be president two times for a total of eight years. Jordan couldn't take it anymore. The barrage of crap coming from the man's mouth was too much.

"Liar!" Jordan shouted, using his cupped hands to amplify his voice.

"Dad. Shush. You'll get us kicked out."

"Criminal!"

"Dad!" Corry said, looking around, wanting the ground to swallow him up, as other attendees turned to look at them.

"Impeach!" Boos rang around them.

"Dad stop, please."

"Motherfucker! Asshole!" Jordan's face was turning red, his vocal cords stood out in his neck.

Corry sat down and hid his face.

"Pedophile!"

Security forced their way through the crowd. Before they reached Jordan, an elderly man in the row behind pushed Jordan forwards. "Goddamn Commie shut the fuck up," he said.

Jordan fell onto the people in front. They were already facing his way. The first punch, from an out of work trucker, sent him staggering back. The second from a retired schoolteacher sent him to the floor. Jordan chipped a front tooth as his face met the rough concrete ground. His nose started to bleed. Supporters on either side of the Stricklers began to pile in. Kicks to his back, legs, head. Jordan brought his arms up to protect his face and instinctively curled up into a ball to reduce the size of the bullseye on him.

On stage, Trump goaded the crowd. Called on them to evict the loser.

Around the Arena the echoing chant of 'Evict the loser' started up. All Jordan could hear above the stomp of feet and slap of fists was 'loser, loser, loser, loser, loser.'

"Corry," he called out as a heavy work boot caught him on the side of his head. Turning his painful, loud, and scary world into black silence.

Corry watched as his father fell. He tried pushing the attackers away, but there were too many, and he was not adult enough to stop them. They pushed him back into his seat, and he watched, tears streaming down his face.

Security eventually reached them, and the crowd dispersed, back to their seats. The large, brown shirt clad, men, picked up the limp body of Jordan and dragged him off the bleachers.

"You better go with him," an older man told Corry. "He'll need you."

Corry wiped his eyes on his sleeve. Stood and followed. He looked at the people he passed. They were shaking their fists and stabbing with their fingers. Wide eyes and screwed up faces. Corry shrank before their rage. These were the people he spoke about with his friends. Calling them patriots and decent, honest Americans. How could they treat his dad like that? The loser chant still rang out, but Corry stood straighter as he realized that his dad was right. These people and their president were scum. Focused on hate instead of truth. Not even questioning because it's come from their side, and their side won.

About the author

Paul Blake

Paul Blake is an English author who identifies as American due to the, quite frankly, ridiculous amounts of American TV shows and movies he has watched over the past forty years.

He is the author of the short story collection A Few Hours After This

www.amazon.com/Few-Hours-After-This-Collection-ebook/dp/B07PZC67JW

and the spy thriller A Young Man's Game.

www.amazon.com/Young-Mans-Game-Paul-Blake-ebook/dp/B07VHS3HFH

In a way, he is jealous of America because the Trump madness can only last for a maximum of two terms whereas the insanity that is Brexit will be here for at least a generation.

"I could stand in the middle of Fifth Avenue and
shoot somebody,

And I wouldn't lose any voters."

Donald Trump - 2016

But They Aren't Bulletproof

By: Shayne K. Keen

It was like waking from a years-long fever dream.

Bill Cushion pulled off the red hat he wore all those years and stared blankly at its stained, yellowing-white screed; those four simple words stitched in breaking thread. What on Earth made him wear such a thing in the first place? It was ugly, it looked wrong on his small head, bulging out at the sides even after being distressed to the point of shabbiness. He looked into the mirror and put the hat on again. He winced and took it off, laid it on the dresser, but hated the look of it there.

He went to the attic and tried to leave it among the bric-à-brac to gather dust along with pictures of the kids and those rough things they made in school that were emotionally valuable but otherwise useless.

Everywhere stacks of dusty boxes leaned against each other. On top of one stack was Steve's old clarinet in a dry-rotting fake alligator-covered case, over which hung a dusty pennant flag from Jeannie's college years, next to Margie's yellowing wedding gown which slowly rotted on a headless mannequin. He touched it, and the lace felt violently fragile, unable to withstand his presence, very much like the one who wore it so long ago, who couldn't bear to be with him anymore, so…. He routed that thought away down the murky river and into the dark mine at the back of his mind.

Atop an old dresser with crackled finish and yet more dust, the hat seemed to leer like a malign ghost. Bill never felt haunted before, not even when Margie died. He didn't feel haunted when the kids stopped talking to him – and oh, even in his most rabid and dark period he had wanted to talk to them. He wanted to forgive them and to beg their forgiveness, but never did they haunt him. The hat haunted him. He grabbed it from the dresser and stomped across the attic and back downstairs.

Bill took the hat outside, started up the grill and threw it on. He expected its cheap made-in-China mostly polyester fabric would melt and probably ruin the grill, but what did he care about grilling? Who did he have to grill for? He looked back over the last several years as the cap sat engulfed in flame, thinking of his son and two daughters. No matter how much he fumed and ranted at them, no matter how much he told them about the wonderful world the president created before their eyes, they were of the adversarial party and would settle for no less than the Great Man's body in prison and his presidency erased.

They got their way and were apparently right in their condemnation. Bill was ready to move forward with his life, admit his wrongs and concede. He was willing to eat every word that he spewed since the man was elected.

"Jesus, this thing stinks," he muttered as he turned the hat over. It wasn't burning for some reason, so he closed the lid and cranked the grill up to high. Surely the heat build-up would set it ablaze.

*　　　*　　　*

Any chance of visiting or even talking to his children was ruined at a Christmas gathering when, during the feast, as FAUX News blared in the living room, his daughter suggested he turn it off – or at least change the channel. He exploded and screamed, "I know you're a bunch of unpatriotic asshole liberals who want to drive the world into socialism, supporting that little German bitch who wants to take away my right to drive my Chrysler," (a '78 Cordoba he'd spent considerable time working on, restoring it to from-the-factory condition.) He saw the hurt, confused looks on their faces but went on anyway. "You're a bunch of libtard snowflakes, just like the ones I hate, so I guess that means..." His mind wanted to stop the reverie. He swallowed hard as the stench from the dark black smoke pouring from the grill made his stomach lurch.

"In a time of healing, the painful memory must be followed to conclusion," he remembered his grandmother saying to him when his father died. So, he let his mind go on. "...That means I hate you. I hate you all! Get out of here!" He swept his arm toward the children's table and continued with, "You sniveling brats deserve to be shot in school if you think the purpose of being an American is to take away my guns!" The fact that he never owned a gun before the election bubbled up from the core. Two months after the swearing-in he bought two, a pistol and an assault rifle. The kids and their families left as one. They never got in touch with him again. He thought of ghosts and hauntings.

Bill opened the grill. The hat was singed around the edges, but that was it. He poked the hat down into the spaces of the cooking grate. It still didn't catch on fire. He left the hat in the flame and went inside to look for something flammable, settling on a half-bottle of Ronsonol left over from when he smoked. He pulled the hat out with a pair of tongs (it was hot, but still not burning), doused it with lighter fluid and put it back on the grate. Flames burst up and roared, but the hat still didn't burn.

"Fucking hell," he said as the flames died down, leaving the hat relatively unaltered. He pulled the hot thing out again and put it on the driveway, went into the shed in the backyard to get the can of lawnmower gas.

He didn't care if it blew up the grill, he was burning that goddamned hat.

* * *

Margie died the year after the election, one of the worst years of his life. They always were political rivals, but it never made much of a difference – until that election. She KNEW. She told him from the get-go that if anyone was the anti-christ, it was that guy. If he won, he would do so much damage to the United States, and maybe even the world itself, that they would never recover from his terrible reign, at least not in their children's (and probably grandchildren's) lifetimes.

"Call it women's intuition," she said a couple weeks before the election, pleading in her eyes. "Please, please, don't vote for that man." That was when Bill bought the hat and started wearing it everywhere to let her know how he felt about her 'women's intuition.'

He scoffed at that, just like he scoffed at everything else the biased, fake media said the President and his group of henchmen supposedly did, just as he scoffed at the Russia investigation, the Mueller Report, and the impeachment. He scoffed at it all, disbelieving any evidence presented, any testimony given. He distilled his rage and impotence into quick, stupid soundbites that made him, and everyone else who used them, sound like morons and fools.

Bill denied the new holocaust going down on the border, even when reporters for the New York Times uncovered the mass graves filled with piles of corpses of immigrants who died in the camps. He called it fake news, and listened to the nightly spin as FAUX gave him the *real* story; the one that didn't hurt, the one in which he was always justified in his hate for those who'd bring down his savior, The King! The King!

He wanted, then, the man to be King! Emperor! A hundred years of his reign! And for what? His taxes went up, the quality of his medical care went down, the high prices in stores made his pension and social security check go nowhere, and he was angry, afraid, and alone. Just as Margie predicted before she died.

At her funeral he cried with his children and grandchildren. They ate together afterward and hugged as one by one they left him to his new, empty life. He told them he hoped they could come together again soon, apologized for having been distant of late, promised he loved them, then waved animatedly as they drove away.

"Traitors," he said as soon as he was by himself. He knew, after all, that anyone who didn't 'get' what the President was saying, what he was about, was a traitorous fuck brainwashed by rampant fake news. His children were as good as terrorists for not supporting the man, who was obviously put there by God to save this nation from itself and its socialist leanings.

That night he grimaced as he thought about them shit-talking him and the President behind his back, judging him unfairly just like Margie did. But he judged Margie for dying and believed beyond any doubt that he was right and she, not to mention their offspring, was wrong. No shade of gray existed between obvious wrong and right. A black-and-white reality of good and evil was all he saw, and its only hope to destroy the blackness and replace it with white and good was that man, slightly orange, who knew what the real American was about. He settled into his easy chair and fell asleep watching FAUX; sometime during the night he woke to see a blonde woman mocking climate change and decided to buy an old gas guzzler to restore.

*   *   *

The hat dripped with gasoline as he put it on the grill. A large fireball engulfed it as he dropped the tongs and closed the lid before it singed the hair off his arms. The temperature gauge went so high that it broke. Bill ran away as the grill rocked and rumbled like something alive was trying desperately to get out of it. He ran inside and called his daughter, Jeannie, the one he'd always gotten along with best. She didn't answer, so he tried the others who, likewise, didn't answer.

After the Christmas debacle, Jeannie had informed him that she, along with her brother and sister, wouldn't visit him again and hoped he would get his papers in order so he could go to the home of his choice if he got too ill to care for himself. They would not be there for him.

He called her again and left a pleading, urgent voicemail full of apologies and promises. He did the same with the others. He wanted them back, goddammit, his children and grandchildren were all he had now. He wanted Margie back, too, but that was impossible.

He took the phone with him and pried open the grill with tongs, being careful not to touch the red-hot handle. It had ceased rumbling, so he was hopeful. But even through the cloud of black, acrid smoke that poured from it in tendrils like a living beast, roiling down the front of the grill and over his feet, he saw red.

"No!" he screamed as the phone rang. It was his son, Steve, who he thought was probably gay.

"Steve!" Bill said, joyfully.

"What do you want? I heard your groveling voicemail and figured I'd better call."

"I don't want anything, just to talk, to apologize…"

"Oh, it's easy to apologize when you're a loser, huh? When everything you stood for is now exposed as the evil, we all knew it was in the first place, even Mom. So now you want to say you're sorry? After calling us names and chasing us out of your house, and on Christmas for fucksakes?"

"I know I was wrong. There's something that happened to me, like my eyes were cloudy, but today they could see again, clearly. I could…"

"You fucking disgust me, old man," said his son. "You supported a genocide, three new wars, and a war against LGBTQ people. You would have let that man kill entire swaths of the population if he hadn't been brought down first, and now you want to apologize? Go apologize to all those South American refugees he had murdered and thrown into pits. Go apologize to all the political prisoners he took from their families and threw in jail who all mysteriously died. Go apologize to Mom, who had to watch you become a monster until she finally killed herself because she couldn't see a reason to keep living."

"She didn't kill herself; it was an accident that she took too many..."

"Keep lying to yourself. I thought you were ready to deal with this shit? No? Well, fuck you and have a shitty day." The line went dead. Bill sat in the yard in front of the grill and cried as it belched smoke, who knows from what – it surely wasn't the hat burning. The girls never called him back.

*   *   *

The trials were long and thorough, and pretty much everyone associated with the administration who didn't squeal like a pig for a lenient sentence was sent to prison. A few people received the death penalty, but the man himself received life in maximum security. That life didn't last long, of course: someone on the inside shanked him within a week. FAUX tried to treat it as a tragedy, but all around the country from Shitstick, Indiana to New York City, there were parades.

Everyone was glad it was over – even his most staunch supporters had long ago bailed, hoping to avoid prosecution, either by court or their neighbors and families. After all, how could *they* have known what was going on down there, how could *they* have known about his ties to Russia and plans to infiltrate the government with Russian operatives? How could *they* have known anything at all?

Bill watched as the new president talked about a Green New Deal, saying the country had a lot of hard work ahead repairing the damage wrought by the previous administration's carelessness and greed. Bill wasn't impressed. He sat in his overstuffed recliner swilling a bottle of Old Crow and wearing his bright red, indestructible hat, and wondered if it gave him superpowers.

He called his son, but no one answered, so he left a voicemail.

"Hey faggot! I hope you die of AIDS before I die of old age, you cock-sucking little piece of shit!" Bill took another slug from his bottle and punched in the number of his youngest daughter, Stella, leaving a similar message but with a liberal peppering of the words "slut" and "whore." He didn't call Jeannie. He just couldn't say anything so awful to her.

"Your initiatives call for lots of tax dollars to go toward repairing the environment. How do you propose to pay for this?"

"Stop asking this question over and over again. My time is limited here, and you are wasting it. With the rollback of the corporate tax cuts that my predecessor so lovingly gave his buddies, we are in great shape. In fact, we are going to be fine. The world doesn't have to end in smoke, fire, and private prisons filled with people who couldn't pay student loans. There's so much work to do and we can do it, all of us, by working together. Good night!"

"Well, this is it," said the blonde Republican Barbie talking head on FAUX, "they have achieved socialism. You know there's only one way to stop it!"

Bill felt his hat tighten around his head as a pulse of electricity zapped his scalp and punched down into his brain. He got his assault rifle and pistol, went into the garage and threw them into the back seat of the Chrysler. Yes, they'd lost, he thought as he pulled out of the driveway and put the top down. But it was far from over. A chosen few would go out to create the kind of havoc promised by the secret words of the Great One, words now released back into the atmosphere with the death of his body. Words only the Chosen could hear.

He drove toward town; already gunshots and sirens, screams of the dying and terrified, filled the air. He grinned and didn't notice when a bullet penetrated his hat and went into his brain and out the back, splattering the rear seat of the Chrysler with blood and gray matter, gooping up his guns. He wasn't really aware of much as his car slammed into the side of a convenience store, and surely didn't hear someone yell, "Well fuck, we got one of our own by accident!" as the last breath and anything else that was Bill Cushion left his body.

About the author

Shayne K. Keen

Shayne K. Keen hails from rural Louisiana but spends most of his time now in Northern Michigan with both cats and humans.

He writes short stories. Poems, and strings-of-words. While not an optimist, he believes things are rarely as bad as they could be.

"The world is not doing well,

and we're going great."

Donald Trump – 2019

Tomorrow is February 13th

By: Scott J. Couturier

The world is a cruel place. Given, there is much in living that is not cruel: yet, cruelty undeniably lurks beneath the veil of our most hum-drum everyday comforts. Every sip of coffee or cigarette puff is underscored by blood-soaked histories of exploitation so monstrous and systemic most refuse to even think about it. Yet, they drink the coffee, smoke the cigarettes, buy the diamonds, upgrade to newer and 'better' cell phones manufactured in Chinese labor camps. In the First World, Everyone Is Culpable: this became my mantra. Did you know they lure tribes out of the Amazon with chocolate made from coco grown on plantations where primal jungle once flourished? They use it to establish trust, then kill the tribe, burn down the forest, and plant more coco.

I have a fragile constitution. An academic, born in Detroit, Michigan: my specialty is Gothic literary criticism. The Brontës, Radcliffe, Lewis, Poe, both august Shelleys. Older, grimmer literature. That was my job. However, I read broadly, generally holing up in my apartment when not teaching, ridden by a debilitating cough. My companion for the past decade, it has grown ever-wetter and hoarser. COPD. Growing up, my backyard abutted a GM plant. Streamers of chemicals used to vent over the lawn...assuredly, my two-pack-a-day-for-twenty-years habit didn't help.

What's worse, the world seemed to be sickening alongside my body. Society going apeshit, friends and family losing their minds, replacing them with something *else*, un-mindlike and malignant. I started to get burning sensations under my skin, like the pincers of bugs. That's when I knew I had to *get out*. Away from the USA, from America and her hungers, the maw of frantic self-delusion-and-consumption. I put in my resignation, cashed out my accounts and bought a plane ticket. I didn't tell anyone I was going to Dresden.

I was going because of Kurt Vonnegut. I'd re-read *Slaughterhouse-Five* recently, and my mind was ablaze with the toga-clad effigy of poor, war-and-time-torn Billy Pilgrim. A bit Intro To Lit, I admit: but, it's a book I revisit often. Every time I read it it feels a little closer to the surface, a little more like waking reality. I remember when it just seemed like a bad dream.

I was going because Dresden had burned down. Germany seemed like a good place to me, these days: still living in the shadow of its own unspeakable atrocities, trying to do better, to stand up and be an exemplar of reformed society. I thought, I can go to a place with no history. Scorched clean, the earth and all its inhabitants charred to a crisp by flagrant flaming holocaust. As my nerves went, I started seeing things – monstrous, unreal things. I thought perhaps misery was opening my third eye. I saw shadows the size of skyscrapers, lurching hungrily across the LA cityscape: they bent and bit into the masses below, ripping off bits of essence, sucking out light and injecting darkness. Colossal life-glutted demons – in Dresden I would find peace. The dead were quiet there, but they were vigilant. They kept such things at bay.

I arrived in a rainy, gloomy October. You'd never guess that Dresden ever burned down. The buildings are magnificent, ancient, or at least ancient-seeming. The lights gleam beautifully at night – the lights Billy Pilgrim never got to see, because the city was on blackout. I didn't speak German, but that didn't matter. In a way, I enjoyed the isolation guaranteed by this lingual barrier. I was here to disappear for a while, perhaps never to resurface: a pilgrim, seeking for the peace of obliviousness. I took lodgings at a boarding house on the city's west side, a place with a centuried air of hospitality. Thick wooden beams, plaster scrubbed to pristine whiteness, high ceilings and a fieldstone hearth the size of a Volkswagen, the works. The owner, Mrs. Weber, spoke a bit of English. She was old, though still younger than the firestorm that consumed the city on February 13th, 1945. She told stories of Dresden's re-settlement, said her house was built over a burned-out garment factory.

My room was on the third floor, an attic space. As I had in the States, I spent much of my time during those first few weeks hidden away: more so, in fact, since I no longer had classes to teach. I'd brought along two duffel bags full of books to pass the time, and got an eReader too (I was disdainful, but caved under pressure of need). The city, of course, offered a smorgasbord of galleries, restaurants, museums, libraries, theaters, vistas, shows, people, *culture*. I went for walks every other day or so, but avoided all the usual tourist haunts, preferring to stick to my local muddy suburb. Sometimes, all Europe seems like a tourist haunt, but that's just the American in me complaining. Americans imagine everyplace else as some kind of theme park. Send a postcard, move on to the next exhibit. No need to tip – everyone's on the payroll.

My rooms were modest. A small bedroom and sitting room/library, a very small entry foyer. A sunroom where I could soak up what little light spilled through the gray, grainy welkin. A kitchen with enough space to cook in (I like to cook). Thrilled by my circumstances, I set about hermit-ing with gusto. I kept far from any news sources (all the papers were blissfully in German), my eyes downcast when I walked the streets. As I'd supposed, no demonic shadows stalked the skyline of Dresden, but there were…other things here. Furtive, small, half-faded things. Gibbering echoes, wailing shades. The ghosts were neither as quiet nor as benevolent as I'd hoped, but their wounds were old and scabbed-over, at least.

Snow started falling early, in mid-November. I thought about Edgar Poe and his 'bleak December'…what was I getting myself into? Surely an iron German winter would break my spirit, my body, or both. But, I'm a Michigander! Snow drifts fifteen feet deep, bitter lake effect winds, no sun for six months, the works. I'd survived it as a child, and I'd survive it now, even with my raspy old lungs. Struggling to squelch a recurrent craving for nicotine, I wondered what terrible black things now prowled the ruins of Detroit.

Detroit, Dresden: cities whose names begin with D. Dead cities, reborn cities. Industrial centers. Hearts torn out. Seven letters to a name. They had a lot in common. I started pulling down the blinds at night.

Weird little blue-gold fires began burning among the buildings of the city at twilight. If I looked down in the street, I saw them lighting up the windows of adjacent houses, or licking up through sewer gratings. They seemed to spread as winter waxed, each night shining a bit more brightly and luridly. Sometimes, I fancied I could hear air raid sirens: dim, barely perceivable wails raising gooseflesh on my neck and arms. The general news wasn't good. Merkel's coalition was fracturing, the European Union in a tailspin. From 2014-15 Germany had taken in thousands of Syrian refugees, sparking right-wing furor in a country dedicated to making atonement for its past genocidal impulses. Hate crimes were on the rise, the barometer of all fascism. I started sweating bullets, tossing and turning in my bed. I'd spent everything to come here, thinking it the safest place...or maybe I'd really just come because of Kurt Vonnegut. I wondered, could I find a meat locker somewhere and seal myself away, safe, from the world?

Each night, I started hearing a heavy *stomp-stomp* coming up the stairs towards the attic. The loft space had been divided up by walls of thin plaster, three rooms in all, and I was the only person lodging on the third floor. The footsteps always ascended around the same time – shortly after midnight, sounding sometimes like the *clomp* of a single set of boots, sometimes like the thunder of a dozen grim-faced shock troops. Whether the steps of one or many, they always jackhammered past my door, on down the hall towards the furthest room. Mrs. Weber said this was used as a storage room, since the chimney took up so much space. Once or twice I asked her whether she ever heard or felt anything odd about the place, and she said, "Nein," urging me in fragmented English to remember that the house, though not as old as the firestorm of '45, was still quite old and prone to making strange noises, especially at night.

I closed my blinds to avoid seeing the fires, but there was nothing I could do to block out the stomping sounds. I tried earplugs, to no avail: the sound almost seemed to come from *inside* my head, echoing outwards. From down the hall I sometimes heard the faintest of pathetic human whimpers, the sounds of people whispering or laughing or singing faintly. The manifestations grew more vivid as winter deepened, and I found myself getting out more and more. I lost myself in Dresden's streets – which are,

almost defiantly, quite beautiful. One Monday I ran afoul of a
PEGIDA gathering – anti-Islamist protesters. They march every
Monday, as it happens. I got out of the way and watched from an
alleyway at the signs bobbing up and down, guttural shouted
slogans and twisted-up faces, teeth bared beneath glassy eyes. I
went out less after that, my rooms now haunted by tiny
manifestations of the blue-green flame.

Despite my best efforts at isolation, I occasionally had
visitors. Hermann Welk, an old man, former engineer and quite
lugubrious: he lived in the room below me, spoke easy English. He
would regale me with tales of Germany's post-WWII industrial
boom, lamenting that the mechanical miracles he was raised to
serve and glorify were now despoiling the world. He'd done his
time among the machines, and preferred living alone in almost the
same level of hermetic seclusion as myself. Perhaps that's why he
singled me out for his attentions. My other visitor was named
Amalia. She was a former refugee, driven from her home in Syria by
the endless civil war. She'd once had a husband and two children,
whose pictures she carried in her purse, but they were all dead
now. She worked at a nearby restaurant, serving schnitzel and beer
to the locals: she endured racial slurs and the occasional sexual
assault. She told me all about it one night in early December, when
the blue-green flames were flaring brightly. Almost I asked her if
she could see them, but – she would have said something if she had.

The winter was gross. The snow didn't pile up, like it did
back in Michigan or upstate CA. Instead, thin and treacherous ice-
crusts formed over everything. I couldn't go for walks as easily,
plus PEGIDA seemed to be demonstrating on other days now, too.
The news from back Stateside wasn't good – I heard whispers and
felt like a coward, having fled my homeland in her hour of utmost
need. Emails flooded in from friends and family: they'd found out

where I was, somehow. I didn't respond. Having crawled deep into my hole, my meat locker, I felt a reluctance to emerge. My mattress was soaked through, rank with sweat.

Well I remember the night. Boots were trampling up the steps, shortly after 1 am – one of those times they sounded like thunder. Through the walls, I heard the unmistakable high-pitched scream of a child. I was seized by instinct and raced to the door, thinking something very real and terrible was happening out in the hallway. So far I'd refused to peek out as the footsteps tromped by, unwilling to give the phenomena a visual inroad. Now, heart pounding, ears filled with a child's terror, I threw open my door and lunged into the hall just as phantom bootfalls crested the stairwell.

A chill – like the blast from an open freezer – flooded my lungs. I staggered and fell against the wall, turning to look towards – whatever it was. Behind me, the child was crying. Other voices joined in, another child's, a man and a woman's. They wept like the world had just cracked itself in half, like hell's gates were yawning open, broiling them with heat. I grit my teeth as I stared into a miasma hovering at the stairhead, *wishing* for heat. My blood congealed, the moisture in my eyes freezing to a slurry. I had to blink away salty flakes.

The blackness had shape and form. It oozed up the steps like a tide of oil in reverse, sending out tendrils of groping void. Red lights flickered in its depth, eyes sans pupil or iris, orbs of backlit blood: hovering around them like a cloud of blasphemous fireflies were iron crosses and silver swastikas, gray eagles with killing wings outspread, the dread lightning insignia of the SS. Even as I gaped the apparition growled and surged forward, my bones shuddering to the *tromp-tromp-tromp* of heavy boots.

It passed through me, chilling me to utmost marrow. It went on, bursting into the furthest room, wood splintering – but, the door remained unbroken. From inside came a renewal of those godawful screams.

I ran to the door. I hurled myself against it with all my strength, again moving on instinct. There were tears of icy blood pouring down my cheeks.

At last the door gave way. I entered just in time to see a phantom band of Nazi soldiers execute the ghosts of four people. *Bang – Bang – Bang – Bang!* The weeping children – a young boy and girl, their heads erupting with ectoplasmic gore – collapsed. The parents slumped over their bodies, mouths fixed in horror, bullet holes gaping between their eyes. I bent over and vomited.

It was then the ghostly fires overcame Dresden.

*

I'm not sure what happened next.

Suffice to say that Amalia found me. Bless her, she'd brought me some hummus and pita bread. She helped me up from the floor (where I'd lain all night – my lungs were hoarse from the cold) and got me into bed, all-the-while demanding to know what I was thinking. I tried to tell her what I'd seen, but my vocal cords were still paralyzed by a lingering cold spot. I shivered and shivered, no matter how many blankets she heaped on me. At last, a doctor was called.

Germany had excellent doctors during WWII. They advanced nascent fields of medical knowledge by experimenting on live victims – Jews, queers, gypsies, immigrants, the usual scapegoats for all society's ills. When my doctor arrived, I couldn't look at him. I fought the delusion that he'd come with my long-lost identical twin, intent on sewing us together.

At long last I slept, and dreamed about Detroit. Decades passed at a furious pace – I watched as skyscrapers were worn down into ghoulish nubs by time, element, and neglect. Yet, there was the lost beauty of Motor City, still alive on time's event horizon. I could hear music. The blues, rock 'n' roll, Motown, jazz, underscored by the growl of proud automobile engines. Germans took to the automobile like naturals, though (of course) the very first experimental car was created by a German. Karl Benz, in 1885, unveiled the Benz Patent-Motorwagen. Several decades later, the necessity of conquering the Michigan wilderness – coupled with the state's native iron supply – spurred Henry Ford to an act of industrialized audacity known as the Model T. Still, the Germans had dibs on the car. Dresden was a major maker of cars before WWII, and still is (in fact). During one of my few day trips in the city I visited the Transparent Factory, an exhibition space operated by Volkswagen. It was refurbished into a 'showcase for electromobility' in 2016: the building lived up to its name, made entirely of huge transparent windows set in a steel-box frame. Coincidentally, the Ford World Headquarters (situated in Dearborn, a suburb of Detroit) is called *The Glass House.* It is made entirely of huge transparent windows set in a steel-box frame.

Detroit, Dresden. Cities whose names begin with D. Industrial centers, makers of automobiles. Hearts torn out: replaced, in Dresden's case. Seven letters to a name. They had a lot in common. Maybe there would be more enthusiasm to rebuild Detroit if it was incinerated, all-of-a-sudden, in a firestorm. Instead, it suffers a long, slow burn – over 3,000 acts of arson annually. And, since the city's bankruptcy, a fire department of bold-but-struggling volunteers making do with worn-out equipment. Sometimes whole blocks burn...I haven't been back to Detroit in years, not since I moved to LA. But, things burn in California too. The very land seems seeded with destruction. Everywhere I go I find fires.

I slept for a long time. After a while, thankfully, I didn't dream. When I woke up my lungs were filled with fluid.

*

One of my favorite stories by the Irish fantasist Lord Dunsany is titled 'The Madness of Andelsprutz.' In it, the narrator tells of a city violently conquered some thirty years ago, its people brought under the reign of a foreign king. As a result, the city's *genius loci*, or inherent spirit, perished, leaving it a husk (though, its inhabitants went on living). Maddened and weeping, the soul of Andelsprutz rose up and fled into the mountains, a self-mourning memory of buildings and mad lights and voices – so our narrator hears from folk in the now-dead city.

Andelsprtuz's ghost crouches and mumbles madly of war in the dark, wracked by grieving. At last, the personified spirits of other great lost cities – Camelot and Babylon, Athens and Ninevah – come to comfort it. The spirit of Andelsprutz is soothed, and at length rises and walks into the distance, leaning heavily and mournfully on Ilion (aka Troy) and Carthage.

So it is a city can die. There seem to be many ways. I've wondered: can the spirit of a species die in the same way? Is there some intrinsic Spirit of Humanity we've lost, a specter of grief and madness haunting Earth's bygone path in the void, howling lamentations to our present depravity? And if so, are there spirits of other great races to come and comfort it?

Is humanity a great race?

Needless to say, I was spending too much time in bed.

The phantasmal fires swept through my room every night. They followed the heavy tramp of boots, the screaming of terrified children, four gunshots. I had been told – commanded – to stay in bed and rest. The doctor gave me some medicine. Antibiotics: at a molecular level all of creation is evolving to destroy us. I refused to take it at first, and developed a fever.

If a city can die but its population survive, can a city's population die but the city survive? What would that look like? I forced myself to get up and potter around.

I hadn't heard any news from the outside. I told everyone it would be bad for my health. Mrs. Weber, good old Hermann, Amalia especially – they all seemed to want me to recover. They talked about small things when they visited. Amalia made sure I was taking my medicine. Christmas and New Year came and went.

The nightly tramp of boots was growing louder, rattling the house's frame. I managed some research from my sickbed – a family of Jews hid in the walls of the textile factory that formerly stood where Mrs. Weber's boardinghouse was built. The story ran a lot like Anne Frank's: Anne and her family were arrested on August 4th, 1944. The family who hid here (name of Weiss) were executed on February 4th, 1945, little more than a week before the firestorm. Incidentally, it is estimated that Anne Frank died in February-March of 1945, at the Bergen-Belsen concentration camp.

These revelations turned my stomach. I started researching obsessively, wondering if I could somehow help the ghosts next door. The world was awash in little blue-green flames. Even during the daytime I could see them burning.

It was surprisingly easy to acquire the needed materials. I sent Amalia to buy them. She asked no questions, though I think some of the objects offended her faith. She visited less afterwards, which was fine with me. I set about learning incantations of exorcism from four different faiths: Catholicism, Hinduism, Kabbalic Judaism, and Islam, with some informed syllables from the *Ars Goetia* thrown in. By night I got up and waited by the door, listening as the black things rushed ravenously past. Long watches were spent girding myself. My lungs were still rough, but I no longer got out of breath when crossing the room.

The little flames were everywhere. They ran along the floor in phosphor runnels, flared ghost-like in my hair. I was waiting until the night of the 4th, date of the Weiss' murder. My researches indicated this was the only night I could hope to make any impact on the endless, horrific replay of events. I spent the day prior etching sigils on the floor, silently hoping Mrs. Weber would forgive my presumption. No doubt my enterprise would force me to relocate, though this wasn't a problem: I wanted to be gone from Dresden before February 13th.

Night fell with an alarming swiftness, almost like the sun was drowning itself. The shadows started stirring in the hall even before twilight settled. I had my book of incantations in hand, needing no light to read by, as the world was effervescent with writhing blue-green fires. How they must have shown in my eyes!

At last I could hear whimpers from the ghost children, the fevered shushing of their parents. A *tromp-tromp* of many boots throbbed up the stairwell, attaining the hall.

I kicked open my door and lurched to intercept, wheezing with the effort. Stark malice confronted me – seething oleaginous witch-oils lit by an underworld of hateful eyes. The pendants of the Reich assailed me, swastikas branding my flesh, the little SS lighting zig-zags sending shocks of static electricity into my vision. Blinded, struck with the pain of a hornet's attack, I managed to warble the words of the first exorcism, right hand scrabbling to find relevant runes on the floor.

A chuckle rolled over me, juddering every cell to its nucleus. My perceptions were wrenched forward. Out of time, out of space – I saw gray fire-lit filaments radiate from Earth in a hoary web of disease, enmeshing the cosmos. My efforts to save the long-dead Weiss family were futile – I couldn't hope to stem the lusts of this entity by mere mortal means. My novice's knowledge of sorcery rattled around dully in my skull before vanishing in a whirlpool of dark ignorance. Resistless, I was conducted to a near-future fated by the will of the fires, saw expanses of faceless, windowless black towers under an ash-jism sky. I was made to understand the air was dense with molecular drones – tiny mechanical motes that pervaded the atmosphere and inhabitants of this too-near future.

Below, someone was fleeing in terror. Black of skin, blue of eye: she clutched a bottle of dirty water to her chest. The drones in her blood migrated to her brain, expending themselves in a destructive chemical embolism. The woman pitched over, blood spewing from her ears and blue eyes. The plastic water bottle rattled along in the grist to roll against my foot.

I beheld a wide world suffused by such self-animate particles. The wave of the future – like light, they were wave and particle both. An AI of immortalized and amalgamated human monstrosity, operating on the quantum level – to be born was to be enslaved to the pervasive atmosphere of a probing and perverse consciousness. If one's infamy matched one's masters, one could join the unholy throng...a ceaseless orgy of proteins, bred and slaughtered by a disassociate fascistic will. My eyes flashed open from the vision. I was covered in flames that burned fiercely, but with no heat.

The darkness surged over me. I was alone in the starveling black, lit solely by the fire licking at my skin and clothing. I heard the Weiss' collective scream – my brain was shivered to unconsciousness by their agony. I heard the usual gunshots, but they didn't stop at four. Instead there was a gain in fire rate, rifle shots turning to machine gun staccato, mortar thunder, bombs falling with whines to detonate deafeningly. I felt myself borne up on a hot, wet, sticky tide, and without seeing knew it to be blood.

*

I fled Dresden the night of February 12th. The flames were everywhere, burning bright in the daylight, outshining the sun but casting cold instead of heat. My lungs couldn't take much more.

Came over Stateside on a redeye flight. Told no one, but left notes for Hermann and Amalia. Looking down into the infinite Atlantic, I saw threads of fire spreading along the seafloor, burning lurid as phytoplankton, revealing terrible secrets of deep rents in the ocean's bed. Flames licked up from our plane's wings, spat tempestuously from its engines. Like a burning phoenix we came in for a landing at Detroit Metro. The city caught the infection of Dresden's flame. Even as I checked into my hotel I saw sparks gusting on the wet, cold winds rolling off of Lake St. Claire. The seven towers of the GM Renaissance Center flickered like huge candles on a cake – by their light I saw the lean, starving shadow-things that prowl Detroit. Towering, thin as utility poles, with no eyes but wildly snuffling noses, they keep low to the ground and root in the wreckage, truffle hunting for stray human souls.

I've wrapped my face in bandages; can't let anyone see the burns. They'd think I was a white supremacist. I checked the news, and now I know everything. The fires flicker on television, on the anchor's sets (though they are oblivious), in every location shot. Outside all I see is a green-roaring inferno.

Tomorrow is February 13th. Tomorrow the bombs fall on Dresden – and the whole world will burn.

"I can be more presidential than any President

who has ever held this office."

Donald Trump – 2017

Thump Trump

By: Paul Blake

He sat up with a start. His heart pounded in his gold Trump pajama top. He stayed still, listening. Only the usual wheezing whine of his chest. He pulled back the gold Trump quilt. The empty McDonald's wrappers with their congealed grease-residue beside him cascaded onto the floor.

THUMP.

He looked around for the source of the noise. Melania wouldn't wake. She was plugged into the corner of the room, updating. He rolled himself out of bed with effort. His foot searched for his gold Trump slippers. He trod on one of the fallen burger wrappers. The cold fat stuck the paper to his foot. He then found his slipper. He slid his foot in, wrapper and all. Then did the same with the other slipper and foot.

THUMP.

It came from the doorway. He shuffled his way there. His wrapper-clad foot slid around in the slipper as he squished across the gold Trump deep-pile carpet, past the gold Trump ottoman, and the gold Trump leopard-skin rug.

THUMP.

Louder, more pronounced. He looked at the heavy wooden door. He missed all the gold fixtures and fittings from his tower. You'd think after four years in the job they'd redecorate your room as you'd want. Melania beeped in the corner. Her update was finished. She'd now go into sleep mode to preserve battery power.

THUMP.

From the ceiling. He leaned back to look. His neck just didn't bend that way. There was a crack at the edge of the ceiling and wall. He watched as it grew larger. It stretched out along the joint, the whole length of the master bedroom. His mouth opened. He stepped back.

THUMP.

THUMP.

THUMP.

Extruding from the wall in the shape of man came three figures. Their bodies were solid and wide and gold-free. They towered over him and surrounded him. A terrible sound assaulted his ears. Like an automobile being dragged upside-down across the highway. A rough sound. Pure anger.

The first wall monster screamed at him.

LIFE.

The second.

LIBERTY.

The third.

THE PURSUIT OF HAPPINESS.

Fingers grew from the block at the end of their arms. One monster extended one and pushed him in the pudgy chest. Not too hard. Not too gentle. Trump staggered farther backward. He was unable to speak. His eyes widened and his balls shrunk in his gold Trump y-fronts at the stone golems in front of him. He could sense the threat they contained.

The second creature balled his block hand, pulled it back and

THUMP.

He fell to the floor with a

THUMP.

The golems raised their stone legs and

THUMP.

THUMP.

THUMP.

THUMP.

THUMP.

Bones splintered, guts splattered, cotton-candy hair scattered. Figures retreated, melding back into the tasteful beige wallpaper-covered wall as if they were never there. Melania remained seated in the corner passively waiting for the Awake command that would never come.

"You had some very bad people in that group, but you also had people that were very fine people, on both sides."

Donald Trump - 2017

Election Day

By: M.D. Parker

I noticed his arm a moment before it all began. I was standing in line at the library doors, he was just across the driveway road from us; him and half-a-dozen others. He had a tattoo on his shoulder. Looked like Shaggy and Scooby-Doo had stopped solving mysteries after having too many Scooby-snacks. Seemed odd, childish even, given the words flying from his mouth. That arm held an aluminum pole with that ugly blue flag flapping at the end. That arm was pumping up and down and up and down. His mouth, and the many others nearby, endlessly chanted about going home. Sometimes the chant was irregular as some of them, mister cartoon dog included, would fire off more direct statements.

"Hey ya stupid bitch, do you not ah-blah, or whatever? Ya know your illegal ass ain't s'pose to be here. This is America bitch; we don't let wetbacks vote. Go back where ya came from and vote there!"

Those were the words that were crawling into my ear like a worm from the bottom of the bottle. Soon as you get to the worm, nothing but vomited trash comes after. It must have been three full seconds I stared at the cartooned stoned slacker on his shoulder, thinking about being raised in Florida before my Mother moved us to South Carolina (and back again when I got pregnant). She got a better job, though she was still worried, there was never any promises when you had to reapply for TPS status every couple of years. Three full seconds I stood with the door handle pulled open while the woman behind me was filming it all with her phone — I think she was live tweeting. Three full seconds before the I saw his face contort into the sort of panic no movie star has ever truly managed to mimic.

Sounds came. Screams joined.

I could hear the scrambling of Scooby and Shaggy's spinning feet before they ran away from the CEO disguised as a chain rattling ghost.

POP POP POP

Was that...? My mind wandered through the next two seconds as if I was in the park for a Sunday stroll, like I used to do before I became too *cool* to hang out with mom. The glass in the door shattered.

POP POP   POP POP POP POP

I think someone shoved me. Or maybe my body chose to ignore the lag of my mind. My knees found the concrete hard enough that my tongue got stuck between my teeth. My eyes closed as I collapsed the rest of the way to the ground. I didn't feel the tears squirt from the corners, I could only feel my tongue, and then the wasp that stung me; got me right in the back of my shoulder. Must be from my flailing arms. I must've made it mad.

POP POP

POP POP POP

POP POP POP POP

The screams grow, and those two seconds faded. Understanding didn't creep in. It blasted through the doors and announced itself with all the flamboyant demands for attention as a failing reality television star. Someone is shooting. Someone is shooting at me, and the person next to me. Someone is shooting at all of us waiting in line.

I heard it. Shot after shot. Did I get shot? It wasn't a wasp. Oh God, I've been shot! Oh God, little Marcus is at the babysitter. He's not even with my mother. Someone help Marcus, please?

POP POP

The concrete is gritty against my cheek, or is that glass? My eyes shut without my control, doing nothing to stem the tidal wave streaming down my face. I've been shot, all I could think was about the growing pain in my shoulder. Was I breathing? Do I move? I can't stay, must get somewhere safe. No! Must stay still. Don't move, he'll not notice right? He... Probably a 'he' right? It's always a 'he' isn't it? I can see him already. I know what he looks like even with my eyes closed. It's louder now.

POP   POP   POP POP POP

My eyes open. Someone is standing there. boots. Sand colored hiking boots, like the ones that mock the combat boots soldiers wear. On the other side of the boots is the quiet man that had been standing in front of me. His English was terrible, and my Spanish has never been that good (much to the irritation of my mother), but I learned it was the first election that he could vote in. I congratulated him, in Spanish – you're welcome Mi Madré. He lay sideways in front of me, his feet still outside the doors. His white shirt now decorated with a starburst pattern all in red. His eyes stared at me; open and wide. Did he blink? Is he still alive?

POP

The left boot steps down on my hand. I can't cry out; he's not looking down. The tears shoot from my eyes, running down my cheeks and dampening the floor, as the bones in my hand crunch between his shots. My eyes close again as he steps away and through the doors. I breathe, somehow managing not to cry out despite the pain and tears. Everything is blurry through the sting in my eyes.

POP POP

The pressure on my hand remains even after his boot is gone. So much screaming. I try to turn my head as my eyes reopen.

POP POP

More shots, but they're going away, I think.

I can see the street and the edge of the curb outside the library complex. I can see Scooby. He's in the middle of the driveway now, at least most of him. He's on the ground too. I can see the eyes of the stoned slacker on his shoulder. Those inked eyes look just as scared. The man's big blue flag is caught partially under his head and is soaking up all the vile disgust that was in him as it leaks out from the side of his neck. His eyes are wide, but empty. I begin to cry anew. Divided we fall right?

I think I hear sirens among the shots. So many shots. So many like the crack of a belt when snapped against itself. So many shots. How long has it been?

POP POP POP POP

POP   POP   POP

There's blood running down my arm, I can feel it. Definitely not a wasp. It burns and aches like I was hit with a flaming hammer. I want to move but I can't. Our teachers always said to stay quiet and still. Don't move, don't attract their attention. If they don't hear or see you, they move on. I have to get to Marcus.

POP POP   POP POP

My last active shooter drill was only two years ago. They gave them to us up until we graduated. My work doesn't do them, but they made you read and sign a piece of paper that explains what they think you're supposed to do. I want to move. I can't even tell if I am crying or not anymore.

More boots. Black boots.

Dark blue pants, maybe even black. Yeah, I think they're black pants. They just ran by. Three sets I think, or maybe two. Everything is blurry; I must still be crying. I'm sorry son. I'm sorry I couldn't keep your daddy around. I know I say it was his fault, but it was mine too. Forgive me son for not being a better mom, but I'm still just a kid too. I tried to show–

POP POP POP POP POP

POP POP POP POP POP

POP POP POP POP POP

I'm sorry, Mom. I'm sorry I lied to you. I'm sorry I stole your bottle. I shared it with some friends from school. You know though, don't you? Is that why you smiled when I was so sick and couldn't go to school the next day? You knew. It's okay, I'm still sorry. I'm sorry for a lot of things. I'm sorry for making you help me with my baby. I didn't know what to do.

There's still screaming. There's moaning, but the cracks of tiny thunder have stopped. Someone is shouting, but this is different. It's like orders, demands for others to do. My eyes are still closed. I try to open them, but everything is moving, hazy, and there are spots closing in making things darker.

Oh God. Please someone help me, I don't want to die. I may be yelling too. I'm not sure. Am I sitting up? Yes, I think so. When did that happen? How long have I been sitting here? I can see my hand, the left one, already swollen and my favorite middle finger is bent different than the others. There are police everywhere. Some people are walking around like drunken cats as the police try to guide them one way or the other. I'm not crying anymore. My tongue hurts. Funny, I had forgotten that I bit it. There's a voice…

"…ma'am, are you hurt anywhere else? Can you tell me your name?"

Is he talking to me? There's an officer talking to a medic, I think. They're squatted down over the man with the blue flag and the tattoo. The medic unfolds a white sheet and lays it across the man. I could hear his last words as the sheet was pulled up over his head. "We don't let wetbacks vote," echoed until muffled by the thin fabric. The words now pooled around him in red soaking the propaganda-blue flag. I guess he was right.

I talk back to them, but I am not sure what I'm saying. The Paramedic that pulled the sheet over Scooby man, is back to back with the one trying to talk to me. I nod that I'm okay before I see the old soft-spoken man climbing to his feet. The people trying to help him are protesting. He swats at their hands as they try to help him with the wound on his side.

"Sir, please, sir. I need you to stay still," she says.

"Por favor, I must…" he says waving his hands for her to step back. He climbs the invisible mountain to his feet, one hand pressed against his side near the center of the starburst pattern on his white shirt. The paramedic speaking to me has stopped and joins the other, pleading with the man to stop and he stumbles further into the library. There's a police officer there now too.

I'm standing, I don't know when that happened. The man pauses at the table they set up just inside the door and slightly in front of the entry to the conference areas, where the set up the machines.

"I must," he says again.

He tries to grasp a pen sitting on the table. The last one that didn't roll off in the chaos. There is another lumpy sheet behind the table. I can see the hand of the freckled man who'd been signing everyone in. I know now.

One of the medics is saying something to me. I'm not sure what it is but I think the Officer figured it out too, because he put his hand out, in front of her. The quiet man's hand is shaking until my hand touches his arm. It steadies and he leans on the table as he signs his name on one the stained sheets. He smiles at me as he straightens up and shuffles toward the first machine. I think I am crying again, but I sign my name and walk to the voting machine closest to him. He nods and I grin.

I can taste the tears as they reach the corner of my mouth. I wipe them away, draw my breath in deep, and standing as straight as I can, cast my first vote.

About the author

M.D. Parker

As a full-time traveler, M.D. Parker calls the Oregon Coast his home base. He, his wife, and two four-legged assistants are writers, bloggers, and vagabonds sharing their adventures and imagination from Everywhere, U.S.A.

Some of his previous works have appeared in online magazines. *The Ghosts Between* is a recently published collection of horror and suspense, and his science-fiction epic, *The Genesis Echo*, is due out this summer, and the prequel, *URP-113* is available now.

You can follow him across the country, and across the web at:

www.facebook.com/parkerwrites

www.twitter.com/MDparkerwrites

www.writeontheroad.com

"I think it is embarrassing for the country to allow protesters."

Donald Trump - 2018

A Line Was Crossed

By: Leland Lydecker

By the authority vested in me as President by the Constitution and the laws of the United States of America, I, Donald J. Trump, President of the United States of America, find that illegal immigration continues to be the largest driver of crime and poverty in our great nation. It has proven insufficient to bar these bad actors entry at the border. In order to restore the United States of America to her former greatness, the undocumented immigrants that have infiltrated our communities must be found and removed.

In light of these findings, Operation True Citizen shall begin July 1st, 2022. In keeping with the new directives of the department of Homeland Security, all civilians of non-Caucasian ethnicity shall be summoned to appear at an Immigration Processing Center for verification of citizenship.

In order to protect the security of the United States of America, the Department of Homeland Security has been authorized to use any means necessary to achieve the orderly and efficient processing of potential unauthorized immigrants, up to and including the use of lethal force. Failure to appear when summoned will constitute a *criminal offense punishable by up to five years in prison and a $5,000 fine.*

Signed this 3rd day of June, 2022,

Donald J. Trump

Fairbanks Police Chief Daniel Herman groaned and rubbed his temples. The directive was grossly unfeasible in a state like Alaska; a significant portion of the population was not only non-white but had been there for tens of thousands of years longer than any of the state's Caucasian residents.

"Hey, Chief!" Herman sighed even more deeply as Lieutenant Eric Lantz puffed into the office, his gut bulging over his utility belt.

"What is it, Lieutenant?"

"Did you see the press release that just went out? We're gonna be part of that, right?"

"If our assistance is requested." The Chief couldn't quite keep his face from betraying the dread the announcement filled him with.

"Why don't we volunteer to assist DHS? I've always wanted the chance to stomp some beaners!"

"How many Hispanics do you think there are in Fairbanks, Alaska?"

"I dunno. Enough?"

"And most of them are in the Army. So good luck with that."

"Aw, what's got you down? Problems at home?" Lantz grinned gleefully. By now most of the department knew that Mrs. Herman had filed for a divorce, and although the news wasn't official yet, the ribbing had already begun.

"Did it ever occur to you that we're immigrants too?" Herman asked, in lieu of rising to the bait. "Lantz– that's Polish, right?"

"And Herman's German. What's your point? Our families have been here for generations. And they came here legally."

"Legally, huh? So that story you like to tell about your granddad smuggling your grandma and her children into the US is just a story, right?"

"That was different. They were in danger."

"So are a lot of these migrants."

"That's different!" Lantz's jowls quivered with outrage. "All the Lantzes married respectably and became productive members of society!"

"Oh, so because your ancestors married US citizens, that makes it okay? Were there anchor babies too?"

"You know what, nevermind. I can tell you don't have a single patriotic bone in your body." The portly Lieutenant waddled out of Herman's office and slammed the door behind him. Then the door reopened, and Lantz stuck his head back in. "And you're a cuck, too!" The door slammed a second time.

Herman sighed and shuffled his scattered paperwork back into a semblance of order. The Trump presidency seemed to have brought out the worst in many of his fellow Americans, from racism to xenophobia to rabid nationalism. He could only hope that the nation didn't tear itself apart before the monster was out of office.

June 6th, 2022

"That's unconstitutional!" Therese exclaimed, slapping the newspaper down on the kitchen counter. "He can't do that!"

"Well, if it's the Orange Menace, that's pretty par for the course," Joe said without looking up from his crossword puzzle. "But Congress won't be able to agree on stopping him, as usual, so he'll get to do it anyway."

"Have you read his... his... *decree* yet?" Therese demanded.

"No, dear. I prefer to at least get to enjoy half my day before finding out which part of the country I fought for is being flushed down the toilet."

"Read this," his wife said, shoving the paper at him. "They're going to round up anyone who isn't white into some kind of processing center. Does that sound familiar to you at all?"

"That can't be right," Joe muttered. "World War II wasn't that long ago. We're still recovering from what we did to Americans of Japanese descent. We wouldn't..."

His words trailed off as he scanned the article. All civilians of non-Caucasian ethnicity shall be summoned to appear....

"Oh no," Joe murmured.

June 27th, 2022. 7:22 am

"Eve!" Nava yelled from the bathroom. "We're done for!"

Eve glanced up from the book she was reading on the couch of their shared apartment. "What happened now?"

"The Supreme Court blocked Trump's executive order and Operation True Citizen, right? It's unconstitutional," Nava said, emerging from the bathroom with her hair in a towel. "But the new

DHS director Trump just appointed doesn't care. They're rounding up people in a bunch of states anyway. Look!"

Eve accepted the phone and scrolled through the article. Protests snarled traffic in dozens of major cities, blocking access to Immigration Processing Centers. The National Guard had been called in to restore order. Riot police and DHS officers separated people of color from the crowd and forced them onto waiting buses.

In Arizona the DHS had already started going door to door in the poorer neighborhoods, rounding up families. They weren't even given a chance to settle their affairs and report to a Processing Center voluntarily.

"Do you think they'll come for me?" Nava whispered anxiously. "I don't exactly look white."

"Don't be silly," Eve replied. "You're just as much an American as I am."

"You know that's not what I meant," Nava said, holding her tanned arm up beside Eve's pale pink one to underline her point. "My dad's family has Hispanic roots, and my mother's side is Greek. None of us look super white."

"They've all been here for a while though, right? They'll be fine. This is about verification of citizenship; people are probably just overreacting. Your parents will be able to show they were born here, and that'll be it. It's not like they're going to be put in an internment camp or something."

"I should call them," Nava said, taking her phone back. "I haven't seen any news out of Philly yet. Maybe I can warn them to lie low."

The roommates listened anxiously as the phone connected and began to ringing. The ringing continued until Nava's mother's cheerful tone came on, directing them to leave a message.

"Mom. It's Nava. Call me. And check the news, okay?"

"Try your dad. You said he always picks up, right?"

This time the call didn't even ring. A robotic voice stated, "The number you have dialed is no longer in service."

"That can't be right," Nava whispered. "That's his number. I talked to him last night."

June 27th, 2022. 4:44 pm

The 99712 Chapter of the Greater Fairbanks Sovereign Citizens gathered over a cooler full of beer and a roast chicken someone had picked up at Fred Meyer. Their meeting place was Dave Waterson's garage.

Dave was chapter leader, mostly by virtue of having a large enough garage to host the gathering and a spouse willing to put up with the noise. Also present were "Chairman" Dan Davis, the brains behind most of the chapter's activities; Jonas "Indian Kyle" Matthews, who was neither Indian (he was, however, half Inuit on his mother's side) nor named Kyle; former infantryman Cory Miller; die-hard prepper Roger Ryland; and Constitutionalist Lee Patterson.

"It's a gross overreach of Executive authority, but this has been a long time coming," Chairman Dan was saying. "No one stood up to the previous overreaches. It's no surprise that presidents have begun to think of themselves as kings."

"America is long overdue for a cleanup," Cory Miller countered. "Overreach or not, you can't argue with that. Right here in

Fairbanks there are shops you can walk into where English isn't the main language spoken. The Founding Fathers would be appalled."

"Are you still bent about that Yupik bead shop on Second Avenue?" Dave asked. "Give it a rest, man. The Eskimos were here long before we were. Freedom of speech applies to them too."

"I don't care what you speak in your home, but English– "

"What were you doing in a bead shop, anyway?" Roger Ryland asked.

"I was looking for something for my wife," Cory retorted, turning red under his scraggly blond beard.

"The point is," Chairman Dan said loudly enough to drown out the beginning of another round of ribbing, "that these are our fellow countrymen– "

"And women!" Indian Kyle added.

"–the feds are preparing to round up and put in concentration camps. Are we going to stand idly by and let that happen?"

"Fuck the beaners!" Lee Patterson shouted.

"I'm not saying we protect any illegals," Dan reiterated. "I'm talking about showing up to register our disapproval and keeping the Feds from grabbing our fellow Alaskans."

"What do people like that contribute to society anyway?" Patterson muttered. "I say let the Feds have 'em."

"Sure, you do that," Indian Kyle shot back. "How's that saying from WWII go?

Then they came for the trade unionists

And I did not speak out, because I was not a trade unionist.

Then they came for the Jews

And I did not speak out, because I was not a Jew.

And then they came for me

But there was no one left to speak out for me.

Who do you think they're going to come for after they finish rounding up all the brown folks?"

"Fuck the goddamn Ki–" Patterson roared, but was swiftly interrupted as Chairman Dan banged his fist on Mrs. Waterson's washing machine, calling for order.

"Indian Kyle's got a point," Dan said when the ruckus died down. "This is how it starts. If they get away with locking up our fellow Alaskans, regardless of how much or little they contribute to society, renegades and undesirables like us'll be next."

"It's no secret that the Feds have no love for the Sovereign Citizen movement," Dave added. "If any of you think you're not on a list somewhere, I'd advise you to think again."

Dave's words were met with a tide of dark muttering, and a plan began to form for the chapter's response.

June 28th, 2022. 4:29 pm.

In the back room of a tea house, the Fairbanks Knitting Club gathered to discuss current events. Organized by octogenarian activist Dana Hall, the gathering drew knitters of all ages and backgrounds, from union welders to stay-at-home moms to college professors and their students.

"I think we're all in agreement here," Dana said. "Something has to be done. We can't afford to sit this one out."

The silver-haired octogenarian's pronouncement was met with solemn nods of agreement.

"What are we going to do, though?" steely-eyed Jenny the welder countered. "If petitioning the courts or our elected officials had any effect, this would've already stopped."

"There are no less than three thousand separate Go Fund Me campaigns set up to fund resistance to the Orange Menace's latest edict, and to provide legal support to its victims. I think that tactic is pretty well-covered," college student Melody Hess added.

"Do we even know where the local Immigration Processing Center is?" Courtney Park asked. "I didn't think Fairbanks had something like that. We're not much of a point of entry."

"It's going to be in the old Kmart building," Seth Smith said, never raising his eyes from the blue scarf he was working on. "A friend of mine responded to an ad looking for temporary workers to clean the place up."

"They can't be expecting many detainees then," Mariah Kowalski mused. "That place isn't that big. And it hasn't been all that well-maintained, either."

"There's the parking lot too," Dana pointed out. "And if they're not building it from scratch, that's probably their best bet in Fairbanks. Seth, how sure is your friend that he's working on the new detention center?"

"It's the place," Seth said, setting down his project. "They don't call it a detention center, though. They're very specific about that. But they're sectioning off the interior into a bunch of little diamond wire enclosures. It's pretty clear what the place is going to be."

"Oh my God, that's awful," Mariah exclaimed. "This isn't way down south anymore. This is right in our own community! I drive my kids to school past that building!"

"Time after time, peaceful protests have swayed the course of history," Dana said. "The time has passed for petitions and legal action. They're already rounding up innocent people farther south. We're not going to let that happen here."

July 1st, 2022. 6:18 am.

"Jesus," Chief Herman muttered as the makeshift Immigration Processing Center came into sight. Any hopes he might have held for a quiet and unremarkable start to Operation True Citizen were swiftly dashed.

Early in the morning on what promised to be another sweltering day, the sidewalk surrounding the old Kmart was already packed with protesters. Some seemed peaceful enough; as Herman flicked on his turn signal and moved to exit Airport Way onto the frontage road, a sleek van bearing Native corporation insignia disgorged a flock of silver-haired grandmas.

Farther down the sidewalk, the resistance looked less cordial. Ski masks. Body armor. Openly carried pistols, hunting rifles, and AR15s. Among the faces that weren't covered, Herman recognized well-known members of the local Sovereign Citizens movement.

The old Kmart building occupied the last lot on the frontage road. A freshly erected chain-link fence topped with razor wire encircled the building and its parking lot, which had been filled with rows of white tents. A single rolling gate with an electronic badge reader allowed access.

Herman found himself vaguely impressed by how quickly DHS had moved; none of it had been there a week ago. Then again, the construction had undoubtedly cost the American taxpayers a pretty penny. And for what?

The gathering made parking along the fence out of the question, so Herman parked farther down the road in the parking lot of the neighboring rental center. Judging by the number of cars already there, many of the protesters had done the same. Interestingly, the department had received no complaints from the rental company.

As the Chief made his way down the sidewalk, he made a point of greeting those assembled and wishing them a good morning. Nothing positive would be gained by making his interaction with them needlessly adversarial. It was his opinion that the department's best bet lay in keeping the tone of the protest as calm and non-confrontational as possible.

Some of those gathered returned his greeting; others looked nervous or downright afraid. A group of obviously terrified J-1 students presented their passports without being asked. The rugged-looking group of men and women behind the banner of the Welders and Metal Workers Local nodded politely; a few saluted him with their coffee mugs. A woman old enough to be his grandmother asked if he was there to stand up for what was right.

"We're just here to keep the peace, ma'am," Herman replied. A part of him wondered if perhaps he should be taking a stand as well.

July 1st, 2022. 8:45 am.

The press arrived, further clogging the access road. Herman dispatched one of the officers on scene to ask them to move.

Meanwhile, the protest had swelled until an impassable barricade of human bodies wrapped all the way around the fence. There were the welders and ironworkers, a knitters' club of some kind, Sovereign Citizens, hippies in tie-dyed shirts, veterans of every branch of the armed services, soccer moms with kids in tow, college students, delegations from dozens of Native groups, and a gathering in suits and ties. (Lawyers? Mormons?)

On the opposite side of the frontage road, next to the concrete barrier that separated it from Airport Way, a vocal group of red-hat-wearing counter-protesters had gathered. Currently, several of the armed patriots were engaged in a shouting match with the anti-DHS Sovereign Citizens. Apparently, there'd been a split over which side they were going to show up in support of.

As more and more people trickled in, Herman eyed the situation with growing unease. There were firearms prominently displayed throughout the crowd, from knitters with holstered Glocks to vets with hunting rifles. Thanks to some of the most permissive firearms laws in the nation, there were probably many more weapons not being openly carried. Technically no one was doing anything illegal–yet. Herman kept his smile firmly plastered to his face, hoping that a calm-yet-visible police presence would be enough to keep the protesters civil and on their respective sides of the street.

Meanwhile, several vans full of DHS agents had been turned away by the crowd. It was probably only a matter of time before he got a call from someone higher up demanding that he clear a path into the facility.

The Chief was chatting with an elderly community organizer when a murmur of alarm rippled through the crowd. He turned just as the department's armored personnel carrier pulled up and officers in full riot gear began to disembark. At the head of the group was none other than Lieutenant Lantz. The driver got on the vehicle's loudspeaker and began ordering the crowd to disperse, but the protesters were having none of it.

Signs were raised and waved violently, and those in front of the group began to link arms.

"What's next, reservations?!" a Native man yelled.

"Papers, please! Papers, please!" the college students taunted.

The chants and shouting intensified, until even the bullhorn couldn't be heard over the racket. Things were getting out of hand fast. Herman covered the space between the group of protesters he'd been talking to and the phalanx of officers in record time, back ramrod straight.

"Exactly what the hell do you think you're doing?" he demanded when he reached the Lieutenant.

"Your job," Lantz sneered. "As of thirty minutes ago, you've been relieved of command. The Department of Homeland Security wants access to this facility, and we're going to give it to them."

"They don't have the authority to relieve anyone of command. And you're not going to do jack shit. See all those weapons? This is a situation for diplomacy, not force."

The confrontation was beginning to draw the interest of the other officers on scene, as well as the protesters. While everyone was distracted, the knitters moved to the rear of the crowd and began zip-tying themselves into a human chain across the gate.

"You're a coward," Lantz spat, stabbing Herman in the chest with a meaty finger. "They'll either respect the uniform and disperse, or we'll give them a reason to."

Across the road, the red hat gathering broke out in cheers and whistles.

"You will do nothing of the sort. You will get back in that goddamn vehicle and proceed *directly* back to headquarters. And that is an order."

"You can either get out of the way," Lantz said, reaching for his weapon, "or get arrested with the rest of the hippies."

Herman's arms were roughly grabbed, but not by his fellow officers. Instead, he found a Sovereign Citizen on his right and a grizzled welder on his left. They linked arms with him and pulled him back into the security of the crowd.

"Get back here!" Lantz shouted. "You are disobeying an order, and I have the right to use force–"

"Do you want to start a firefight here?" the Sovereign Citizens' leader asked. "You'll look real heroic, firing into a crowd full of noncombatants and children."

"You wouldn't dare," Lantz snarled, but it was clear that the small group of officers was no match for the number of armed civilians present.

Across the road, some of the patriots appeared ready to back up the police. Others seemed to have realized there was somewhere else they needed to be and were shuffling rapidly out of the line of fire.

"And you! You're an officer of the law. You're going to stand with the criminals?!" Lantz demanded.

"This isn't about verifying citizenship and you know it. This is about singling out certain types of Americans and finding an excuse to lock them up. This is how things like the Holocaust start."

"I'm just following orders."

"'Just following orders' didn't cut it at the Nuremberg Trials, and it doesn't cut it now. We both have a responsibility to disobey unlawful commands."

"Arrest him!" Lantz snapped, leveling a meaty finger at Herman's chest.

The riot officers approached, Tasers trained on the Chief and his would-be protectors.

"You may take those of us in the front," one of the Sovereign Citizens yelled, "but there'll be twenty more behind us ready to open fire!"

The officers hesitated. Fat beads of sweat rolled down the Lieutenant's cheeks like misplaced tears. Then: "Fall back!" Lantz barked. "Get the tear gas. If they want to play hard, we'll play hard too!"

July 1st, 2022. 6:04 pm.

"And here's Aaron Chalmers with the news!"

"Thanks, Joanne. Our biggest story of the day comes directly from the Mayor's Office. In a surprise press conference, Fairbanks City Mayor Merideth Wallis declared Fairbanks, Alaska, a sanctuary city. In her official statement, Mayor Wallis said that in light of the overwhelming community opposition to Operation True Citizen, the City of Fairbanks is officially withdrawing its support for the directive.

"Mayor Wallis went on to quote Chief of Police Daniel Herman, saying that 'obeying orders is no excuse for perpetrating crimes against humanity. It is our duty to stand in opposition to unlawful directives, as many of our brave citizens have done today.'

"The Mayor's statements come in the wake of an appalling use of force by rogue elements of the Fairbanks Police Department. The actions, including the unauthorized use of tear gas, were aimed at dispersing a large group of Fairbanks residents who had gathered to protest the opening of the Department of Homeland Security's Fairbanks Immigration Processing Center.

"Not only were the officers unsuccessful in removing the protesters, the tear gas caused several of those present severe respiratory distress, among them elderly and well-loved community activist Dana Hall. Paramedics were called to the scene and found Hall unresponsive; she was pronounced dead at Fairbanks Memorial Hospital. Friends and family say Hall knew the risks of going to the protest, but that she passed away doing what she loved– making the world a better place.

"In related news, sixteen Fairbanks police officers and one Lieutenant have been suspended for taking unauthorized actions and use of excessive force. A confidential source stated that the complaint centers around the unauthorized use of tear gas, which caused multiple injuries, at least one fatality, and also drifted into a nearby residential area."

*   *   *

"We did it!" an ironworker crowed, slapping Herman on the back as the newscast playing on the Chief's phone came to a close. "We really did it! We stopped 'em!"

"For now," Herman said, looking around at the tired, sniffling, red-eyed gathering that still surrounded the Processing Center gate.

"It's still happening in other places, though, and they'll probably try it again here too."

"When they do, we'll be ready," Chairman Dan said.

About the author

Leland Lydecker

Leland Lydecker is a writer, professional driver, and airline hazmat specialist. No stranger to the ins and outs of government and corporate corruption, his preferred writing topics are crime, extra-judicial justice, and the future of society. His first novel, Necrotic City, was published in 2017.

You can read more of Leland's writing at www.lelandlydecker.com

Or find him on:

Facebook: www.facebook.com/lelandlydecker

Twitter: www.twitter.com/leland_lydecker

"THE RIGGED AND CORRUPT MEDIA IS THE
ENEMY OF THE PEOPLE"

Donald Trump - 2019

First News:

America's Truth Network

FORMER PRESIDENT ARRESTED FOR SEX CRIMES AND TREASON ON THE BACK NINE

January 24th, 2021

1:30 p.m.

This report would normally start with the words "shocked" and "never before" and "unprecedented" and while some of these words still apply, the world was not as shocked as one might expect. It was shortly before 10:00 a.m. Eastern time when a series of vehicles driven by agents from the Federal Bureau of Investigation parked on the street in front of New York's famed Trump Tower. At the same time another group of matching SUVs crossed the entrance threshold to the grounds of now former President Trump's Florida golf resort, Mar-A-Lago. Donald Trump, golf club in hand, was taken into custody on a variety of charges including child sex trafficking, obstruction of justice, and more.

Many had speculated from early in the investigations that were conducted by the Department of Justice and the office of the Special Counsel, about what may or may not happen if, or when, Donald Trump could ever be charged with a crime. That speculation reached a fever pitch as Democrats in the House began an Impeachment inquiry as the leaves began to turn in 2019. The vote for Impeachment was blocked nearly a half dozen times and the process was stalled and stonewalled when it finally reached the Senate. Many around the country were frustrated, angry, at the perceived inaction, while others thought it a glorified attempt to swing an election in their favor.

All the wondering and frustration has ended now. The questions have been answered as Donald Trump, his personal attorney, former Mayor Rudy Giuliani, his son-in-law Jared Kushner, former white house advisor Stephen Miller, and his son, Donald Trump Jr., along with several of their associates and staff members were arrested by agents from the FBI. In all 27 warrants were served and 19 people were taken into custody on a yet unspecified number of charges. The range of charges is what is truly stunning: charges of obstruction of justice and abuse of power related to the events in the Ukraine, which many had been expecting after the release of 3 different voice recordings of the President became public. But it was the addition of crimes related to illegal government contracts, acting as a foreign agent, racketeering, blackmail, witness tampering and intimidation, and multiple charges related to sex trafficking and sexual assault that grabbed everyone's attention. The latter charges possibly stemming from the still progressing investigation surrounding the one-time friend of the Trump family, the late Jeffrey Epstein, known colloquially as the "billionaire pedophile."

The Epstein case took several unexpected turns after his death. Though many felt the chance of him naming names of who took part in, or assisted, in his child sex ring had died with him, the ongoing investigation into conspiracy and fellow conspirators yielded mind-numbing results. As the second half of 2020 heated up, many previously unassociated names became entangled in the controversy. Political figures, major business or media moguls, or other well-known personalities were brought in revealing a larger crime ring than few had believed. However, despite numerous allegations and conspiracy theories, former Presidents Clinton and Trump's names had not been announced – until today. While Former President Bill Clinton was not arrested, he was brought in as a "person of interest" according to sources familiar with the wide scope of the warrants and arrests.

Noticeably absent from the arrest warrants were the names Melania Trump, Ivanka Trump, Eric Trump, and the near estranged daughter, Tiffany Trump. For a specific list of each person and each charge in which they were taken into custody for, please click here. Sources from inside the White House have stated that the President is expected to brief the nation regarding these matters sometime this evening. It is expected that this situation will be her first primetime address from the oval office. We will bring you all the details and continue to update this monumental developing story as new information becomes available to us.

About the artist

Daniel Sauer

Daniel V. Sauer is a graphic designer and artist living in Oregon. After years of experience at newspapers, print shops and various design agencies, he struck out on his own in 2000. In 2016, he co-founded (with editor/publisher Obadiah Baird) *The Audient Void: A Journal of Weird Fiction and Dark Fantasy*, which features his design and illustration work.

Since 2017, he has worked extensively on book covers and interior art for Hippocampus Press. His art often takes the form of surreal collage and photomontage, as pioneered by Max Ernst, J. K. Potter and Harry O. Morris.

In 2020, besides appearing here, his illustrations will appear in *Vastarien: A Literary Journal*, as well as in projects published by Weird House Press, Gehenna & Hinnom Books, Hippocampus Press and Audient Void Publishing.

His work can be seen at:

www.DanSauerDesign.com

www.DanSauer.crevado.com

www.facebook.com/DanSauerGraphicDesign

Acknowledgments

First, and foremost, we would all like to thank you our readers for coming along on this ride with us. It is a crazy, hectic world out there, and we can never express our gratitude enough that you took time to spend in our worlds.

This project took a great deal of work in a shortened amount of time to bring to you, which means we have many helping hands to thank for their assistance. In no particular order the authors of Trumpland: Divided We Stand would like to give a special thanks to:

MeLisa Parker at www.writeontheroad.com, Ben Garvey, William Tea, Donald Armfield, and every single friend, family member, and significant other that we have ignored while we worked; thank you for forgiving us for our obsessions.

WE
THE
PEOPLE